CW00402443

Dedicated to those who have struggled, or are still struggling, with mental illness. You are not alone.

"In an attempt to learn more about what happened during a lobotomy, Freeman tried performing them with the patient wide awake, under local anesthesia. During one of these procedures, Freeman asked the patient, while cutting his brain tissue, what was going through his mind. "A knife," the patient said. Freeman told this story with pleasure for years."
—Howard Dully, My Lobotomy

CONTENTS

X

1. Do not resist government efforts to cure the sick of mental illness.

2. Do not attempt to hide your symptoms of mental illness and always seek treatment immediately.

3. Peacekeepers must be obeyed at all times for the good of the collective.

4. Anyone suspected of sickness and exhibiting signs of unsafe behavior must be reported immediately.

5. Citizens are encouraged to watch one another and report any unsafe or unhealthy behavior.

6. Citizens must devote themselves to being of sound mind, hard-working, and cooperative members of the collective.

7. No misconduct is permitted, such as disobedience towards peacekeepers, failure to perform societal duties at home and in the workplace, and/or unsafe relations between unmarried persons.

8. Citizens must attend regular self-curing sessions.

9. Citizens must comply to the mandatory, annual mental health tests.

10. Those who violate these terms and exhibit

signs of the sickness, or unsafe behavior towards themselves or others, will be arrested and administered the cure for mental illness.

.1

SABINE—

The wind was strong that night, wrapping the fabric of my gown tight around my legs. I struggled to keep up with Rory as she strode confidently ahead, apparently unfazed by the possibility of getting caught.

"Don't be a coward, Sabine," she reminded me. It was a thing she liked to say often, her eyes full of fire. "Just act natural and no one will suspect a thing."

I wanted to believe her. I wanted to be brave like her, a girl with eyes full of fire. Instead of the cursed girl I was, spreading bad luck wherever she seemed to go.

We were too young to be here. The age of admission was nineteen, but we certainly weren't the first underage teenagers to sneak into the Beaumont Gardens for the annual bride market. Plenty of people did it and got away just fine.

At least, that's what I told myself, as we slipped

our way in through a gap in the hedges, a rogue twig snagging at my dress and scraping my leg.

No one tried to stop us—no one seemed to notice. We blended into the crowd almost too easily. The ease of it is what made me nervous. Maybe I had been secretly hoping our plan would fail and we'd have to return home, where it was safe. Maybe I really was a coward, but I kept my head high and I tried to act like I belonged.

I couldn't stand to disappoint Rory.

She'd singlehandedly saved me from a childhood of solitude with her bluntness and beauty, and she'd never treated me like I was invisible— like I was my twin sister's less interesting shadow. Even though everyone else seemed more than content to do so.

For that reason alone, I wanted to be a good sport tonight, for her sake. Even though I already knew I would hate every minute of it.

But it was going to be her big night. Because Sofian had returned.

Sofian who'd lived next door to her for years— the same Sofian she'd loved all her life and sworn to marry one day. Older and sophisticated, with amber eyes and rich bronze skin, he'd come back from school abroad just in time for this year's bride market.

Rory wanted to snatch him up before it was too

late, rules be damned. So what if she was a few months shy of nineteen? She wasn't about to stay at home and let another girl have him.

In the heart of the gardens the open courtyard was packed, almost impassable. Tents lined the perimeters, emanating the rich smell of tea, food, and alcohol, and the air was full with bittersweet melodies making promises they couldn't keep.

Our heels scraped against the cobblestones as we squeezed our way through, bumping shoulders in our eagerness to secure ourselves a spot. Eyes sought us out as we went, but I knew they weren't looking at me. They never were, not with Rory standing near. The gown she wore tonight was a silky blue that moved on her body like water, and it was difficult not to stare as she breezed past, her minty eyes and blonde hair glowing as if shining from within.

My gown, on the other hand, was a shapeless-looking thing. A thick fabric so black I looked like a cutout version of myself. I'd worn it as a sort of disguise, since it was sure not to stand out. It was already difficult enough being a natural redhead, in a society where the color red had grown to represent mental illness. I'm not even sure it had been intentional, or if it had just sort of evolved that way naturally. Whatever the reason, red had been virtually erased from our clothes and our homes.

Just not from my own hair follicles—that resilient and shiny copper which sought to betray me since birth.

Where Rory attracted stares of envy and admiration, I attracted looks of vague scrutiny. As though the world somehow knew I was cursed, just from one look at me.

Thankfully, no one appeared to be looking me at all that night, so I assumed the dress was working.

"I don't see him," Rory fretted, her head whipping from side to side as she scanned the sea of faces.

I wondered how she wasn't making herself dizzy. I was about to tell her to slow down, when she came to an abrupt halt in the center of the courtyard. I nearly crashed into her, catching myself just in time.

Then my eyes instinctively followed her line of sight.

There, only a couple of feet away, stood the unmistakable George Maize. His tall figure loomed easily above the crowd, and the powerful boom of his voice carried across the cobblestones, crashing against us.

Rory shuddered with revulsion at my side, quickly snatching my wrist and dragging me into the opposite direction.

I concealed my face so she wouldn't see me

blushing, as we cut a path through the crowd and ducked into one of the tents, pulling aside the curtain to reveal a teahouse bathed in warm candlelight and scratchy music playing over old speakers.

We sat on a bench and each ordered a cup of tea, while I forced aside any lingering thoughts of George.

Rory wouldn't stop fidgeting.

"Stop looking over your shoulder," I said. "Sofian will turn up soon. It's still early."

"It's George I'm worried about. I hope he didn't see us."

"Even if he had, I'm sure he has no reason to talk to us today."

She nodded and let out a deep breath, visibly trying to calm her nerves, although I could tell it was a wasted effort. Even after our order came, she couldn't keep her eyes off the door.

I tried telling her not to worry. Sofian's family already knew her well, and this was his first year at the bride markets, so the chances of him picking someone else were slim. But my words seemed to go right over her head.

"I'm sorry." She smiled sadly. "I'm not good company tonight, am I?"

"Don't worry about it," I said. "I get it."

I didn't mention just how badly I understood, since the thought of George finding someone tonight made me sick to my stomach. But I couldn't say that to Rory. It didn't matter that George's brown eyes were bottomless or that he towered taller than any other man, the sheer size of him dividing a crowd like a mountain. It didn't matter that he commanded the attention of everyone around him simply by existing, with his undeniable charisma and charm. These things I had to keep secret, because Rory would probably knock me over the head with a stick if she found out.

She'd never bothered to hide her dislike of him. Sometimes, I thought she might even have hated him.

"Men like that are the worst kind of men," she'd said about him once.

"Men like what?"

"Loud," she'd said, scrunching up her nose, as though it were the worst possible thing a person could be.

.2

RORY—

Sofian smiled at me as he left the teahouse, amber eyes shining, his hand reluctantly letting go of mine. At the last second, my fingers clutched air, and just like that it was over. The night was coming to a close.

My eyes dropped to my hand, to the card now clasped tightly in my palm, the edges sharp. Sofian had slipped it there discreetly. I read the inscription over and over, not quite believing it was real.

Sofian's family name was embossed into the thick paper, and I ran my fingertip across, imprinting the words to memory.

Sofian Hunt.

This card was a silent promise. A promise I would belong to him. All I had to do was hand the card to my parents, and the transaction would be complete. Rory Renaud would be sold.

It was exactly what I'd wanted, what I'd always dreamed of, and yet the longer I stared at the card, the harder it became for my lungs to fill with air. I swallowed, trying to force down the rising panic, all the while sensing the eyes in the room pressing into me.

Sabine's eyes, too, as she watched from her nearby seat.

I didn't dare look at her. This is why she'd come tonight. She'd broken the rules—she hated doing that—just so she could be here and witness all my dreams come true. How was I supposed to explain to her that I suddenly didn't want them? How was I supposed to answer her questions? I couldn't even answer my own.

Uncertainty was an unfamiliar sensation. I was used to moving through life headstrong and sure of myself, and now here I was, choking on doubts. It made me feel pathetic.

I was the girl who was never afraid, how could I suddenly be so terrified of something I was so sure I'd wanted?

My feet inched towards the door of their own accord, my body craving distance.

If only I could make it away from all these people and get a few seconds to think. If only I could get away fast enough, then I'd be out of sight before Sabine would have the chance to catch up to me.

Somehow, facing her seemed like the worst

thing of all.

"Rory?" I heard her calling, her voice moving closer.

Another wave of panic hit me, and I didn't stop to think things through. I launched myself at the door. I heard Sabine behind me—a choked sound of surprise—but somehow it propelled me forward, instead of drawing me back.

The night air hit my skin like a soothing balm, welcoming me in its grasp. The stars had vanished overhead, replaced by a thick blanket of humidity and electricity, and I wanted to get lost in it. To wrap it around my body like a comforting veil.

I ran into the night as fast as my legs could carry me in my platform shoes. Around me, the courtyard blurred, the tents and the trees reduced to shadows. I didn't stop moving until the chaos of the bride market was behind me, and I found myself standing at the entrance of the famous Beaumont Labyrinth, its wrought iron gates calling.

It wasn't recommended to go in alone, especially not at night, but I pushed through anyway. I was the girl who laughed in the face of fear.

Or at least, I had been, until tonight.

I found a spot to kick off my shoes so I could run freely through the grass. The paths were lit by the soft glow of lanterns, casting jagged shadows across my face, and the labyrinth felt so welcoming—so deserted and peaceful.

No one would bother to venture in here at this time of night, not on the day of the bride markets. There were more important things to be done, wives to be bought.

I felt grateful for the solitude as I raced through the winding maze, holding up my skirt with white-knuckled fists. I didn't slow down until I was good and lost—until I felt like nothing could catch up to me here. Not even that horrible feeling I'd felt in the pit of my stomach as I'd held Sofian's card in my palm, the sensation that I'd done the wrong thing. In the labyrinth, all that mattered was the rapid drumming of my heartbeat, the delicious burn in my muscles, and the gentle presence of shadows brushing against me like friendly ghosts, as though offering encouragement.

I stopped running once I felt like my lungs might burst and like my heart might beat its way out of its cage. Which, coincidentally, happened to be the exact moment when the sky opened, and a loud crack split the night. A violent downpour came crashing down, soaking through my gown in the seconds it took to find cover under a tree.

"Rory?" a familiar voice called.

I whipped towards the sound, startling when a large figure materialized and loomed above me in the dark. I hadn't heard him approaching. The downpour must have drowned out the sound of his footsteps.

George Maize.

I gaped up at him. He really was a giant. It wasn't often that I needed to crane my neck to look people in the eye, especially while wearing heels.

He said nothing at first, and only the sound of the storm filled the silence, that thick blanket of rain hitting the soil all around.

My initial reaction was shock, quickly followed by an inexplicable rage. I braced myself, expecting the worst. It was no secret we'd always hated each other.

George pinned me with a pair of dark eyes, his hair dripping with rain, his chest rising and falling rapidly from his run. He looked wild.

"Did you follow me in here?" I asked.

"Yes."

He took a step forward. I took one back. I was afraid again, although I didn't know what I was afraid for. My life? Or was it something else?

I clenched my hands into fists, nails digging into my palms, trying to stop the shivering. My whole body felt like it was vibrating, and I wasn't convinced it was from the cold.

"Do you want me to leave?" he asked, voice clapping like thunder.

I winced. He was always so loud. That was one

of the many reasons I hated him, he was always just too damn loud.

And I did hate him, didn't I?

"No," I said, although as soon as I said it, I couldn't believe that word had just come out of my own mouth.

He leaned closer. "Are you really going to marry him?"

Was it his close proximity that shocked me, or the question? Maybe both.

I instinctively shrunk backwards, losing my footing against a root in the ground. In a rush, George's arms went around me, saving me from the fall and leaving us awkwardly entangled, pressed up against the tree like a pair of ridiculous lovers.

Under different circumstances, I would have laughed.

Just not this circumstance.

George's arms held me upright, and yet I had the sensation I was still falling—crashing—spiraling down some long, forbidden path. My hands crashed against his chest, as though trying to keep him at a distance, in more ways than one, but he was like a stone wall against my palms.

He made no further move. I knew I was free to step away. And yet his eyes bore down into mine, and he looked... what? What was I seeing? Anger?

Desperation?

"I don't want to end up married to a stranger," I said, but it sounded like a poor excuse, even to my own ears.

"But we're not strangers, are we?"

A new kind of panic raced through my bloodstream. We'd never acknowledged anything aloud before. It was the unspoken agreement between us, and it seemed wrong of him to suddenly change the rules.

"You're going to marry someone else, too." I lashed out in anger, since that emotion felt safer, more familiar. "Isn't that what you were doing here tonight? Getting your family to buy you a wife?"

He smiled, a flash of perfect white teeth in his dark face. "And that bothers you, doesn't it?"

My hands faltered against his chest, as though they had a mind of their own, caught between pushing and pulling. George's arms tightened around me, and all at once, I was helpless. Helpless in the face of his helplessness. One of his hands grazed a patch of bare skin at my back—a caress, a gentle assault. I didn't stand a chance.

I hated that he was right—hated him more than I could possibly say—hated him so much that I was breathing hard and couldn't think straight. My thoughts felt disjointed and nonsensical, and the whole world had disappeared, everything reduced to a single instinct.

"What is it?" he whispered.

"I have the most awful feeling," I whispered back.

.3

SABINE—

S tanding in the labyrinth where I'd attempted to follow Rory, the rain was coming down hard and my shoes were sinking deeper and deeper into the soft grass, but I couldn't move. I was transfixed, my eyes glued to the two figures standing in the dark, their silhouettes bending towards each other.

Before I knew it, he was kissing her. Softly, like asking a question.

I was trembling, but I can't say I felt cold. At least, not from the outside. My outside had gone numb completely. It was my heart that was freezing over inside my chest, my blood crystallizing in my veins.

George was kissing Rory. Rory was kissing him back.

I was momentarily too stunned to look away, even though I knew it was wrong to be watching them. They could be arrested for something like this. I would be expected to report them, as a witness.

Rule number 7: No misconduct is permitted, such as disobedience towards peacekeepers, failure to perform societal duties at home and in the workplace, and/or *unsafe relations between unmarried persons.*

I should have turned away immediately.

Instead, I stood there like a fool, and it wasn't until George's hands were moving to other places that I finally had to walk off.

My dress had become plastered to my body—my fingers and toes had grown fuzzy and disconnected. I walked off in a daze, struggling to draw air into my lungs, my feet stumbling blindly through the soggy grass.

The rain was relentless in its assault, sheets of it coming down at an angle, and it felt like a small eternity of mindless wandering before *they* found me.

I'm not sure I would have made it out of the labyrinth if they hadn't. I might have walked in aimless circles forever. They seemed to materialize from the shadows, their threats splitting the night like steely blades.

"Stop right there," the first peacekeeper shouted, flashing a light directly into my tear-streaked face.

My feet stuttered to a halt and I squinted into the beam, white spots burning into my retinas. I could barely make out their black coats from behind the light. It took me a long second to count them.

Three peacekeepers.

"Can you show us your identification?"

I knew it was against the rules to refuse, but still, I shook my head. I was caught off guard, my thoughts turning to mush. My first instinct was denial: This couldn't be happening.

We'd never had a lot of peacekeepers in the small, often overlooked, collective of Reye. Even on the night of the bride markets, there were only a few stationed in the courtyard.

It didn't make sense to come across three at once.

My mind raced, wondering what would happen to me now—wondering what the punishment was for underage teenagers sneaking into the bride market.

I had a feeling I was about to find out. One of the peacekeepers stomped closer, reaching towards me with a black-gloved hand, and I braced myself.

"Leave her," one of the others interrupted. "She's not what we're after."

I should have felt relieved by his words, but they only brought on a new wave of fear. What were they after, if not rebellious teenagers breaking the rules? Something worse?

I didn't dare ask. It was probably better, not knowing.

With the recent incidents we'd all seen splashed on the news, it wasn't hard to imagine the many possibilities. There were rumors of changes coming, of the cure for mental illness becoming mandatory for everyone, even those who were healthy, and a lot of people were protesting.

Not all the protests had been peaceful.

"It's awful," Rory had said, when we'd watched some of the broadcasts on her smart-wall at home.

Someone had been standing amidst protestors outside a curing clinic, holding up a sign. In angry bold letters, it read: *To do nothing is to be an accomplice!* Then a second later, they'd dropped the sign to swing their fist into someone's face, and we didn't hear the crunch, but we saw the gush of blood.

Rory's face had gone pale. She must have been thinking of her big sister, Corinne, who was a healer. One of the medical professionals responsible for administering the cure, in a clinic much like the one on the news at that very moment.

"Violence can't be the answer," Rory had whispered in horror.

Remembering those broadcasts, that's suddenly all I could picture. A fist going into a face, a broken nose gushing with blood. Had people started protesting here, in Reye? The protests had seemed far away, when we were watching on our screens at home. They weren't supposed to happen here.

I probably would have remained where I was—paralyzed with confusion in that labyrinth during a rainstorm—if it hadn't been for the peacekeeper who grabbed my elbow.

"I'll take care of this," he spoke to his partners. "You go on ahead without me."

"If you're sure."

The peacekeepers exchanged swift nods, mechanical tilts of their heads, then we split into opposite directions.

We walked for what felt like a long time, especially since I was cold and miserable and didn't understand what was happening, but I was strangely grateful for the peacekeeper's presence. At least he seemed to know the way out, and he hadn't arrested me yet, so maybe he hadn't figured out I was underage.

The only problem was that he was urgently rushing me forward with an iron grip, and I could barely keep up the pace, my shoes slipping on the slick surface of the wet grass.

Something was definitely wrong.

"What's going on?" I asked.

The peacekeeper peered sideways at me through the darkness. "Did you say something?"

It wasn't a talent of mine, being heard. It was a skill everyone except me seemed to have. They didn't even try, they just had it, while my voice failed me time and time again, coming out too soft—too weak. The more I resented it, the weaker it became, as though spiting me.

I repeated the question, struggling to make my voice heard above the rainstorm.

"We have to evacuate everyone," he answered.

So, I was right after all. "There's really been an incident? In Reye?"

That's what they were calling them on the news: *incidents*. Ever since the invention of the cure, we'd had no use for the word violence—it had existed only in history books—and reinstating it into our vocabulary now must have felt too much like admitting defeat.

Not that it really changed anything. Violence was still violence, even when you called it by a different name.

"Not exactly," the peacekeeper said, which only confused me more.

If not an incident, then what? I had no idea what else could warrant an evacuation, and the peacekeeper never stopped to explain. He simply plunged us deeper into the night, further through the winding maze.

When we finally reached the exit, he pulled us to a stop.

"It should be safe for you that way." He pointed into the middle distance. "Make sure to get home as quickly as you can. A kid like you shouldn't be here in the first place."

My heart nearly stopped in my chest, faced with a new reality: He knew. He knew I was underage.

And yet he was letting me go.

I blinked at him, trying to figure out a way to say thank you. In the glow of a nearby lantern, we saw each other's faces clearly for the first time. It wasn't considered polite to stare at a peacekeeper, I'd never dared to before, but in that moment, I couldn't help myself.

I already knew he was cured. All peacekeepers were. It was a requirement when working for the government. What I didn't expect was that you could see it, the emptiness left behind. Like a dark tunnel where their eyes should be.

I shuddered, wondering if this is what being cured truly meant.

When I still didn't move, the peacekeeper raised his arm and pointed into the distance again, his voice dropping low. "You have to get home now. Everything will make sense later."

He was giving me an order. I had no other

choices left.

Numbly, I nodded and turned away, facing the rain and the darkness on my own. In the brief instance that I glanced behind me to check, my savior had already melted back into the shadows.

0

1. ~~Do not resist government efforts to cure the sick of mental illness.~~

2. ~~Do not hide your symptoms of mental illness and always seek treatment immediately.~~

3. ~~Peacekeepers must be obeyed at all times for the good of the collective.~~

4. ~~Anyone suspected of unsafe behavior must be reported immediately.~~

5. ~~Citizens are encouraged to watch one another and report any unsafe or unhealthy behavior.~~

6. ~~Citizens must devote themselves to being hardworking, cooperative members of the collective.~~

7. ~~No misconduct, such as disobedience towards peacekeepers, failure to perform societal duties at home and in the workplace, or unsafe relations between unmarried persons will be tolerated.~~

8. ~~Citizens must attend regular self-curing sessions to ensure health and wellness.~~

9. ~~Citizens will comply to mandatory, annual mental health check-ups.~~

10. ~~Those who violate these terms and exhibit unsafe behavior towards themselves or others will be detained and cured at the curing clinic.~~

1. All citizens must receive the mandatory cure for mental illness.

1

L ife is different now. Now, we sit around the dinner table like carefully arranged orna-ments. Me, my stepfather, and the peace-keeper who's moved in with us, as though we're pretending to be a regular family—as though we're puppets tied by silver strings thin as spider webs.

No one speaks. Not with a uniform always around, watching, listening.

When the government passed the new law en-forcing all citizens to receive the cure, peace-keepers stormed into Reye. Truckloads of them rolled in like thunder, and all households were ordered to give up their spare rooms for the peace-keepers and healers.

The first couple of days, life halted to a stand-still and any resistance was handled with force. People were put under house arrest to await their curings—forced to be prisoners within their own homes—while more incidents filled our televi-sion screens, footage of the black coats in their riot gear pushing back the crowds.

The monsters are no longer just in storybooks, they're right here in our faces—sitting across the table from you, cutting into their steaks with sharp knives. *The peacekeeper is under your bed— he's in your closet,* children whisper, a flashlight held under their chins.

I peek at the peacekeeper while we eat, trying to make sense of what I'm looking at. I can't decide what's more terrifying, seeing the peacekeepers on duty or off. Their eyes just don't look right. You have to really look to see the difference, but it's there. That emptiness I've come to recognize —their surfaces smooth and polished, their smile lines not as deep.

This peacekeeper's hair is a metallic blond, shaved close on the sides, and his eyes are blue, which doesn't seem like an intimidating color at all. In fact, up close, his face isn't directly menacing, which strikes me as odd considering the reputation attached.

I've already heard so many awful rumors.

It used to be only the sick that got cured. We would get tested every year, a routine appointment. If you showed signs, they'd give you the needle, and then forever after everyone would wonder what you did—how sick you were to deserve it.

That doesn't matter anymore. This is an epidemic, and we are being quarantined.

"Is all of this really necessary?" my stepfather's voice interrupts our meal.

I hold my breath, fork clutched in fist.

The peacekeeper barely reacts, still cutting into his steak with meticulous precision. "It's for the protection of everyone. These are dangerous times."

He has a soft-spoken voice, but somehow, the fact he never yells is worse. He glances up and stares at my stepfather with his steely blue eyes, as though daring him to speak again, while the setting sun shutters through the blinds, casting long strips of light across his stony face.

There is something about his mouth, I notice. Something about the way it presses firmly into a flat line, which suggests there is *more*. There has to be, otherwise it wouldn't make sense, would it? How else would there be so many awful stories about him? Stories of families being sent to the rehabilitation centers, or of children being permanently separated from their parents, all in the name of some promised safety.

I wonder what he'll do to us. If we put one foot wrong, I wonder what he'll do.

2

On the day of my curing, the peacekeeper escorts me to the clinic for my appointment. I know I'm one of the first citizens in my collective to be scheduled for one, but does that mean the government has noticed I'm cursed, or is it just a coincidence?

Somehow, I don't think it is.

The peacekeeper hovers at my back like a shadow, the heavy stomp of his boots inadvertently urging me forward, and yet, I feel strangely calm as we walk through downtown, the glassy fronts of the buildings watching me with their vacant faces, the weak sun beating down through a thinning layer of cloud.

Is it wrong of me, to feel relieved?

I didn't expect relief, but now that my curing day is here, an unavoidable end drawing closer with every step over white concrete, the cure seems like a small mercy. A promise I won't end up like my mother or my sister—a promise the curse will end with me.

I only start to feel uneasy when my shoes hit the tile floors of the clinic. The smell of citrus burns into my nostrils—oranges and lemons, a common scent for self-cleaning spaces—and immediately reminds me of a simpler time.

There's something about scents that can make you remember things, and for me, the tang of citrus in the air will always be tied to the memory of school. My school days with Rory were some of my best times, and I'd give almost anything to be back there instead of here right now, in the chilling air conditioning of the clinic.

But school also reminds me of George. His face always comes up—square jaw and dark eyes, memories of him in the classroom or on the playground, towering above everyone. I can perfectly recall his booming laugh crashing over me like a wave, knocking me sideways, and I have to push the thoughts away, out of pure self-preservation, to focus on the task ahead.

The smart-walls of the clinic flicker at us as we pass, flashing with advertisements and soothing images. At the end of a long hallway, a man smiles from behind a pristine desk of shiny white marble, but the smile never reaches his eyes. He wears a healer's uniform in a soft and faded blue, and I wonder if they make the uniforms that color because they imagine it to be soothing somehow?

It doesn't feel soothing now.

"Welcome, Sabine," the healer says, his voice kind and comforting, but in a rehearsed way.

Does he notice my copper hair, flashing an angry red amidst all these muted colors? It feels especially inappropriate here, for some reason, as though intentionally defiant. Does he find it offensive?

He shows no sign of being offended. He simply hands me a slice of smart-glass, cool against my palms. At my touch, the screen of the smart-glass illuminates with a lengthy document, and I press my fingertip wherever it's needed—an electronic signature.

I sense the peacekeeper looming from behind me, watching over my shoulder. Can he sense how badly I want to run? I think he does. He presses closer, as though to warn me not to try.

I hand back the tablet of smart-glass and watch it disappear behind the desk, before I'm motioned to a side door.

There's no wait time. The healer steers me away, and my feet falter of their own, my stomach twisting with a sudden knot of nerves—this is too fast, too confusing. Helplessly, I glance behind me at the peacekeeper, as though he might help—his job is to protect me, isn't it? But his face is a blank mask, his blue eyes cold like ice, and with a sharp tug at my elbow, I'm forced into motion.

I have the sensation of being dragged towards

a cliff, and an involuntary whimper escapes my throat as I cross the next threshold, the door hissing shut behind me, sealing me in. I'm brought to a surgical room with a single operating chair and given instructions for where to look, how to hold my head. The healer positions me just right and puts the straps in place; his hands are freezing, leaving goosebumps wherever they touch.

He secures the head piece with a snap, so I'm pinned down, and panic grips my throat. I force it back before I throw up.

The room offers none of the relief I had stupidly imagined earlier. Instead, there are only questions. Will I be the same after this? I try not to think about it. My only job is to stare at a focal point on the wall marked by a red dot, and the machine will do the rest.

As soon as the healer exits the room, the lights are dimmed and the procedure begins.

The machine comes to life with a soft purr and a rush of hot air that tickles upon contact. It moves over my skull like a curious animal, sniffing and probing, shifting into place through the use of tiny flickering sensors. My hands clench around the plastic armrests, and when the needle plunges into the soft tissue of my eye socket, I smash my teeth together so hard it's a mystery they don't immediately shatter.

It's not painful. Not exactly. It happens too fast

to feel the pain. But you can sense the intense pressure as the machine moves in a series of clicks, needling its way to the frontal lobe of my brain and cutting away the parts of myself that cause the sickness—the mental illness.

There's nothing to do but sit there in submission, listening to the wet sound echoing within my skull—the sound of brain tissue being shredded. Might as well be the sound of evil expunged from your soul—or perhaps it's the sound of your soul itself, being carefully extracted, like a frightened pet coaxed out of hiding. It slips out and floats above you like a phantom, snapping like a sheet hung to dry on the breeze.

I stare hard at the red dot on the wall, rigid in my seat, praying for this to be over soon. Until suddenly, there is nothing. No chair, no red dot, no machine. Like a curtain dropping over my consciousness, I fall.

3

In my dream, I stand above a girl asleep on the white tiles of a bathroom. Her hands and feet are blue, the digits curled and stiff. Her lips are a discomforting shade of mauve.

She wears my face, and my own eyes stare back at me, frozen wide open, cloudy like a cured person.

I push against her chest, like they taught us in school, but give up quickly. I know I can't save her. I'm like a ghost sobbing over her physical form, wishing I could climb back in, make my soul stick again.

Except it's too late. There's an empty pill bottle next to the sink.

Even as I'm dreaming, I'm aware this isn't a dream. It's a memory. It's from the day I found my twin sister, Sara, on the floor of the upstairs bathroom in our old house. Except her copper hair looks drained of color, and her olive skin has turned ashen. Even her eyebrows look like they're peeling off—like they've turned into crow feathers, likely to float away on a breeze.

My sadness is a cloud of mist all around, clinging like steam to the mirrors.

"Why would you do such a thing?" I ask.

In answer to my question, she wakes with a wild gasp, her head turning, dead eyes blinking frantically, like a glitchy machine.

"Don't let them take it," she says.

That's when I realize the face has changed. It's not mine anymore, but Rory's instead, her mauve lips curled softly in a haunting smile.

"Take what?" I ask.

"Your humanity."

△△△

Coming to after your curing feels a bit like being pulled from under water. One moment you're drowning, the next you're not. The heart pounds and the lungs wheeze—the eyes burn when they open. Life pulses back into your bloodstream, and you can hear it in your ears, that thunderous *whoosh whoosh*. The rhythm of the living.

I recognize my cotton bedsheets, even though I don't remember leaving the clinic—don't remember being brought home. Visions from the procedure flash behind my eyelids, like the lingering effects of a nightmare.

What have they taken from me? What pieces of myself have been ripped out?

I search the fuzziness in my head but all I find is a black hole, gaping wide and threatening to suck me in, while images of Sara on the bathroom floor are still clinging to my peripherals.

In real life, I hadn't tried to revive her. That was just the dream, trying to fix what I wish I'd done. The guilt coming to visit, as it often does. That heavy pang in the chest, always there to remind you of what you did—or, more accurately, what you didn't do.

Before the guilt has a chance to overcome me, something beeps nearby, drawing my attention. Through a brief assessment, I notice an IV in my hand and a monitor at my bedside, displaying a heart rate. *My* heart rate. The machine ticks softly in tandem to my mounting panic, proof I'm still alive.

I don't have time to notice anything else before the door of my room opens with a swish.

The woman who enters seems surprised to find me awake, if you can call it that. Her face is so serene it's hard to tell. She strides into the room carrying a slice of smart-glass tucked into the crook of her elbow, her eyes quickly scanning the screen.

"Sabine LeRoux," she reads. "We're doing another round of house calls this morning. I'm happy to see you up."

She speaks as though reciting a script, and she moves fast, like someone with no time to waste, making quick work of the IV and the various sensors taped to my body, ripping them off like band aids and ignoring when I wince.

Then she slaps a strip of medical tape over the IV mark on my hand. The tape is coated with a layer of sticky medicine, which tingles as it repairs the puncture wound, but it quickly grows hot, dangerously close to pain. I have a hard time focusing on anything else, so I only catch bits of what she's saying.

"You've been out for a while—very common, perfectly normal—" She collects the pieces of medical equipment and packs them neatly into a large black case, then she slams it closed.

I flinch. I can't help it. Everything sounds too loud—heightened. I attempt to ask questions, but even though I can get my mouth open, my throat feels too dry to form words.

If she notices me trying to speak, she never shows it.

"Drink plenty of fluids." She thrusts a water bottle in my direction. "Talk to your peacekeeper if you experience any complications."

In my confusion, I scarcely manage to hold the bottle. I grip it only half a second before it falls and rolls off the side of the mattress.

I watch it disappear over the edge, so by the time I look up again, she's gone.

Helplessly, I stare into the empty space left behind, the ghost of a presence still lingering. Seconds or minutes tick by as my mind floats away, as though detached—as though it were a balloon tethered by nothing but the finest of threads.

The medical tape on my hand snaps me back to reality. It has started to cool at an alarming rate, and soon it feels like a stabbing pain, stabbing through my hand like an ice pick.

I rip the tape off and rub the patch of cold left behind, trying to restore its normal temperature. When I inspect the wound, nothing but a faint mark remains. This is definitely not the typical kind of medical tape you'd find at the store.

I toss the offensive strip aside and go looking for the water bottle over the edge of the bed. I have to sip carefully, since my throat constricts from disuse, but within minutes I can feel the fuzziness clearing from my head. Encouraged, I drink greedily, draining the bottle of its contents so I feel well enough to try standing.

Besides feeling the room tilt, my body seems to respond normally as I push to my feet, so I make my way to the shower on shaky legs and then into a fresh change of clothes. I'm undoubtedly slower than usual, my body a little detached and unfocused, but I manage to get the tasks done.

On my way to the kitchen, my stomach grumbles, and it's a relief to feel something as familiar and normal as hunger. Although a part of me wonders if I shouldn't be feeling different. Isn't there supposed to be some kind of change—some kind of distinction from before the cure?

In the kitchen, I stand at the fridge—a monument of shiny steel in the midst of a very white kitchen. There's a screen embedded in the fridge's surface displaying food options, and my stomach grumbles again at the thought of cereal, so it must still be one of my favorites.

Another thing, unchanged.

The heavy footsteps of my stepfather come around the corner just as I'm settling in a chair at the kitchen island. He enters carrying an empty mug, stopping to rinse it in the sink.

"Thought I heard something," he says. "Glad you're up."

Nothing in his voice suggests a reason for alarm, so maybe there's nothing wrong with me after all. I relax a little as I start to eat.

"How long have I been out?" I ask between bites.

He shrugs. "A while."

I gulp my mouthful. How long is a while? I wait for him to elaborate, but he says nothing. He just gazes at me mutely—neutrally. Once he blinks, that's when I see it. The small incision mark over his eye, like the one on my hand. A puncture wound that's been treated.

He's already been cured.

I look away quickly and stare into my cereal floating in its bowl of milk. That's a bit how I feel right now, like I'm floating in milk.

"Are you almost ready to go?" he asks. "We've got church today."

I nod without looking up, afraid of my expression.

He drifts out the kitchen without another word, presumably to get dressed, and although he never was a chatty man, this new kind of silence chills me.

Kid, he used to say. *Let's go, kid. Aren't you ready yet, kid?*

I hated that, but now it seems wrong without it.

We've never been close. We don't even belong to each other—there's nothing in our blood connecting us—but after mother died, he kept me and Sara. He didn't send us away. He promised he never would, although I believe that promise was mostly meant for my sister. It might be unfair to say he liked her more than me, but that's how it always was with Sara. Everywhere she went, people were drawn to her, the treasured gifted child who was good at anything she put her mind to.

Meanwhile, I was reduced to nothingness, standing next to Sara. Like flying too close to the sun and being incinerated. She was always the most interesting thing about me. Maybe even more so, now that she's dead.

You can't compete with a dead person.

Rory is the one who's always saved me from fading away and becoming invisible, and without her in my life, I might slip into nothingness again.

The nothingness crawls beneath my skin like an itch, and with a sudden impulse, I grab the first piece of technology within reach: a tablet of smart-glass sitting in its charging dock on the counter. We keep it here for recipes or reading the morning news.

It's no bigger than a book or heavier than a slice of smooth, pristine glass in my palms, but it's one of the most sophisticated pieces of technology in the house. With access to everything from the appliances to the security system to the room temperatures, it's like a remote control for the home.

The surface lights up at my touch, recognizing my fingerprint. I quickly open the messaging app using my personal ID and pull up my last conversation with Rory. *This one was from before*, my mind compartmentalizes. Everything falls into two categories now: before or after my curing.

An old conversation glows on the screen like a warning. *Mine's a real pain*, Rory had written, talking about the peacekeepers. *But I hear you've got one of the worst.*

I know, I'd replied.

His reputation had preceded him. People said awful things, and that's all I worried about those first days after their arrival. Even if you did nothing wrong, the peacekeepers made you nervous.

I hate to think what would happen if ours saw this conversation, so I quickly erase all evidence of it and focus on writing something new.

I'm up, I send. Just in case she'd want to know I'm okay. Followed by, *are you around today?*

Then I clutch the tablet in a tight grip, waiting for a response or at least a notification the message has been received. I try not to jump to conclusions, but my pulse betrays me. It knows tragedy follows us everywhere—it's learned to expect it around every corner.

My scalp prickles with a familiar heat, my internal alarm going off, as I stare dejectedly at the screen for long minutes, the blue glow burning into my retinas.

No notification comes. She hasn't read it.

△△△

I hesitate outside the door to the office. When we're at home, this is usually where the peacekeeper is, working on things he never bothers to discuss with us.

I feel like a child being called to the principal's

office, and I consider turning back, but he probably already knows I'm here. He's heard the footsteps; he can see my shadow under the slit of the door. I have to knock.

On the other side, the peacekeeper is bent over his desk, the walls around him thick with books. He's silhouetted against the wall-sized window at his back, the smart-glass set at half-tint, casting us in a dusty light. Somewhere above, the air exchanger sighs, almost inaudibly, sucking the dust from the room.

I approach cautiously, a small shiver tickling the back of my neck, as though there's a spider there. I stop in front of the desk, hands held behind my back, nerves tight in my belly.

"Thank you for coming to see me," he says, not bothering to look up from the slice of smart-glass in his hands. He has it on privacy mode, so the glass isn't see-through from my end, but the glow illuminates his features, tracing the sharp lines, painting his skin a soft shade of digital blue. "I heard you were up and wanted to know how you're feeling."

"Fine," I say.

"Speak up, please."

"I said I feel fine."

He nods. "Well then, we'll be leaving shortly for church, as scheduled."

"Yes, my stepfather said."

A beat of silence as the peacekeeper stares at his screen, squares of light illuminated into his eyes, in place of where his pupils should be.

When I don't leave the room like I'm supposed to, he slowly looks up again. "Was there something you wanted?"

"I was wondering if I could take the car out?" It seems ridiculous that I have to ask for permission, but this is our reality now.

"We always walk to church." The walking part is important, like a preparation for what's to follow.

"No, I meant after."

He's staring at me now, making me feel like I'm guilty of something—like I've been caught red-handed. "What for?"

"To visit a friend." *To check that Rory is okay.*

"It's not safe right now, you know that."

"I know, but—"

Before I can finish my sentence, the peace-keeper is shaking his head at me. My words trail into silence.

"Things have gotten worse," he says, "in the weeks since your curing."

At the word *weeks*, my face nearly cracks from the effort to keep it still.

"There have been some complications. Not everyone is cooperating like they should. It's better if we stay here for now, and try to avoid venturing out for unnecessary reasons."

"Are we in danger?"

He shakes his head at me. "Speak up, please, Sabine."

I repeat the question, louder this time, bringing the sounds forward with a forced, conscious effort. "Are we in danger?"

The word *danger* comes out a hint too loud, the smallest trace of panic embedded in my voice.

"It's just a precaution. It's better if everyone stays in their homes right now."

"Is that normal?" I ask. "That it's taking so long?"

Those eyes of his narrow, blue like the uniforms the healers wear, and I notice they give off the same effect: a discomforting intention to soothe, no matter how unsootheing the presence.

The guilty feeling worsens.

"Are you sure you're feeling alright?" he asks.

"What do you mean?"

He shakes his head some more. He does that a lot, it seems like, especially at me. "If you're tired, you should rest."

"I think I've been resting enough." The word

weeks is still ringing in my ears.

His eyes snap up and I immediately know I've said the wrong thing. He smiles for the first time since we've met. It's a false gesture, and although well rehearsed, it pinches all around his mouth and his eyes.

The smile transforms him. I feel the room shift, and suddenly it all makes sense—it all clicks into place. Him, the rumors.

The smile says, *I am dangerous.*

"You should go get ready," he says. "We'll be leaving shortly."

I know a dismissal when I hear one, so I turn feebly and march out of the room, while a deep inner instinct rises to haunt me: *Something's wrong.* I can feel it, the wrongness. It lives inside me, slithering like a snake, wrapping around my organs. Tighter and tighter.

4

We go to church on foot like we're supposed to, all of us from the neighborhood crowding the sidewalks, walking with practiced unison beneath the shade of the trees.

There is something about the walking that is meant to unite us—to humble us. A reminder that we are all tethered to the earth by the same gravity.

The leaves rustle overhead when the wind blows, as though softly laughing, and the pavement burns white under the morning sun, leaving shiny blobs behind my eyelids.

All the streets in my neighborhood look the same, each side like a mirror-image of the other. The houses are perfect cubes of white with wall-sized windows in shimmery panes of smart-glass, reflecting us back at us when we walk by. We are projected onto them, people-shaped reflections with the peacekeepers hovering closely at our backs, moving like an army of prison guards, urging us all forward in a slow march, legs scissoring to the beat of a silent drum.

My stepfather looks at me, and I'm struck again by the new emptiness in his dark eyes. "You're not feeling faint, are you?"

I shake my head, not trusting my voice.

"That's good," he says. "I did, after I woke up."

I still say nothing. Truth is, I expected to feel different—to feel some sort of physical change, confirming that the cure has worked—but the air today is soft and the sun is warm, and I feel completely normal. At least physically. Which seems wrong somehow, but I don't say that out loud.

As we approach, our little church is a triangle of windowless black steel, rising on the horizon like a sharp and jagged mountaintop. It fills quickly on Sundays, people lining up at the doors. The inside is all dark wood, thick and ornate like chocolate.

Once we're in, we stand huddled together in the pews for morning prayer, tapping the side of our hands with our fingers, heads down and eyes closed. At the end we say, *I accept fully and completely*. It's supposed to be a form of self-curing.

The peacekeepers remain in the aisles and at the doors, like bodyguards. They look strangely ominous; all of them standing tall in their black coats, like messengers of death—like crows. It makes our tiny church feel more cramped than usual.

After we're permitted to sit, the choir files onto the stands. The shiny grey robes of the singers contrast the dark walls, and I believe it's meant to make them look modest, and therefore holy, but they've always looked so flat and plain to me, like aluminum paper. It seems disrespectful, like they haven't bothered to dress right for the occasion.

The singers assume their places, and straight away, I notice there are holes in their formation. It's impossible not to notice, like a smile with missing teeth. I search the faces, trying to find Rory, but she isn't there. She's one of the holes.

I grip the edge of my seat as they begin to sing, their voices coalescing into a well-rehearsed melody, the vibrations rising high into the peaked ceiling. Even though I try, my hands won't release the bench, fingers curled inwards in a way that's sure to lodge splinters into my nail beds. I'm not sure I breathe once during the entire first song, and my head starts to pound from the lack of air.

When the next song starts, my stepfather nudges me, so I remember to light a candle. This is the curing song, the one that's meant to remind us to be good and peaceful, so we won't fall victim to the sickness. They want us to be grateful for the cure.

Those of us who have lost people to mental illness are meant to walk down and light a candle in remembrance of our loved ones.

I'm special because I get to light two.

My knees wobble on the way down the aisle, and I swear I can feel eyes pressing into my back like thorns. Maybe it's just my imagination, but I flush hot all over.

Being noticed isn't something I'm used to. Despite the treacherous red hair, I've always been otherwise easy to overlook, which is something I've taken great comfort in. I'm not even sure why. My twin sister never seemed to have this problem, when she was alive. People were naturally drawn to her.

It's like she was structured differently, despite being made of the same stuff.

I wait in line for my turn. There's a wall of candles, all laid out in neat rows, and they give you a match. My hand shakes and someone steps on the backs of my shoes. I whip around and meet a pair of cured eyes, brown and foggy like flat puddle water.

"Sorry," the girl says. "I didn't see you there."

I breathe a sigh of relief. Maybe I really am imagining things.

As I return to my seat, I try to spot Rory's parents in the pews. Maybe she's there with them, maybe I'm making stuff up in my head and nothing at all bad has happened.

But then I spot them in the crowd of faces, their heads turned towards the front, freshly cured and stiff as robots.

Rory isn't with them.

5

Outside, the afternoon has broken with a hot and unforgiving sun. As the church empties in a slow current, I scan the faces for Rory's parents, but I've lost track of them in the crowd.

I'm about to give up when I spot someone else.

"Sabine?" My stepfather notices when I stop in the middle of the sidewalk.

"I'll be right back," I say.

The peacekeeper starts to object, but I break away and walk straight into the street, cutting across to the opposite side, seized by an impulse.

Up ahead, amidst the crowd, is the unmistakable tall frame of George Maize.

I push past the confused looks and frowning faces. I'm going the wrong direction, like a soldier stepping out of formation, singlehandedly ruining our carefully planned parade. I don't care. I walk fast, drawn in by a magnetic pull.

Perhaps it's my many failed attempts not to

think of him that have somehow conjured him, like some cruel trick of fate. Perhaps it's a sign, or a test.

Either way, I can't help myself.

George doesn't see me coming. He's got his back turned, his peacekeeper at his side, headed towards home. The peacekeeper looks laughably small next to him, just a little man in a little black coat, not to mention terribly unthreatening. At least, in comparison to my peacekeeper, which makes me wonder, not for the first time, why I've been assigned one of the worst.

What is it about my family that marked me as a bigger threat to society than the tall and assuming George Maize?

There are no answers waiting on the sidewalk, but they aren't what I'm chasing. I don't even know what I'm planning to do or say as I cut a path through the mass, all I know is I need to speak to him. Now.

I'm breathless by the time I reach his side.

"Wait," I call. "George, wait."

As though in slow motion, he stops, turns, and blinks. His dark eyes settle on my face and I feel their weight. He's even better looking than I remember. Although I think this every time we meet, don't I? It's like the first time all over again, that gut-punch feeling.

Despite the fact I've clearly just chased him down the street, he looks calm and collected. Muted to the world, like my stepfather—like everyone else.

I don't know why I expected anything different, but the revelation comes as a shock.

He's not looking at me, I realize. He's looking straight through, as though I'm hardly even there —as though I'm just a shadow of a person, standing next to my sister, being incinerated.

Something collapses within me, something not unlike defeat.

The truth is George and I were never really friends. We were only friends by association. But now it's more than that: we're reduced to complete strangers.

All at once, I wish I hadn't chased him. None of the comfort or familiarity I was seeking is here.

"Sabine," George says, voice flatter than the asphalt beneath our shoes. "What is it?"

I attempt to recover. "Nothing, sorry. I only wanted to ask—"

"Yes?"

"I was wondering if you'd seen Rory?"

He shakes his head. "Why would I?"

The sun suddenly feels even hotter, boring down on me like an accusatory spotlight. The top of my head burns, like my red hair might catch on fire.

"I just thought you might have," I say. *You, of all people.*

He shakes his head softly before walking away, the tiniest of puckers lodged between his eyebrows. I watch him go, feeling lost and abandoned on that sidewalk, wondering what's happened to all the people I used to know.

It's the peacekeeper's hand that lands on my shoulder, snapping me back to reality. I shudder at the feel of his touch and cower beneath the weight of his steely eyes, feeling small and insignificant, guilty in the face of my disobedience.

"We're going home," he commands in a low voice. "Now."

I obey. What choice do I have?

We walk back to rejoin my stepfather in silence. This time, it's not just my imagination: people really are staring. They watch the cursed redhead girl cowering beneath the heavy hand of the unforgiving peacekeeper, like mental illness itself being escorted away.

It isn't until we're home, safe from prying eyes, that the peacekeeper takes me aside.

"I think we should postpone your return to work," he says. "I'm going to schedule a follow-up appointment at the clinic."

My stomach drops. "What for?"

"Just a precaution," he says, and coming from him, the words sound like a death sentence.

6

The clinic still smells the same, the morning of my check-up appointment. Citrusy and clean, as though it could wipe your mind of impure thoughts. Every couple minutes, one of the smart-walls of the waiting room flickers and illuminates a name, attached to a room number.

All heads turn to look.

It's not my turn. Someone else gets up and walks out a side door.

Frustrated, I close my eyes and press my hand to my temple, hoping to repel the beginnings of a headache that's been plaguing me since I arrived.

It doesn't help that I'm wrought with nerves, although I try not to let it show. Being nervous doesn't seem like the kind of thing a cured person does.

The waiting room is full today, everyone packed in soft plastic chairs. None of us are here on urgent appointments. The curings still take priority, they're dishing them out by the hour, but the rest of us are here for regular stuff. Check-ups, like me.

It's been twenty minutes now and my name still hasn't appeared on the wall, and with every second that passes, my headaches grows worse. I have to squint beneath the harsh lighting.

Across the aisle from me, one of our neighbors is sitting with his head slumped, not looking too good either. His cheeks are flabby and pale like egg whites, as though he might throw up at any moment, and I tuck my feet inwards, just in case he decides to get sick right on the floor between us.

He lives on my street. Three-doors down, in a big house all by himself. I search my brain for his name.

Toma, I think.

He looks up, as if I've said it out loud. Our eyes connect and his are tired looking, sunken in. At first, it's just a simple glance, vacant and meaningless, but then our gaze continues to hold—he won't release me—and there's something increasingly pleading about his eyes, like he's silently begging to be saved.

I feel a pang of alarm. I can't help him. If anything, I would only make things worse. I always do.

I quickly turn my eyes to the black of the floor. The tiles look so shiny and seamless, you'd think you could fall straight through.

I wish I would. I don't know how much longer I can sit here with this headache, while the overpowering scent of citrus chokes me softly.

As usual with the scent citrus, the memory of school was first in my mind. It's only after sitting here for a while that my head begins to throb steadily, and I'm hit with a second memory. It rises to the surface out of nowhere, sudden and vicious, catching me off guard.

I'm remembering my curing.

I can remember walking out of the operating room on the arms of two medical assistants, and how it felt like I was floating, like it didn't make sense for my legs to be transporting me. The assistants left me in a small, separate room where the lights were low and soft music played over invisible speakers. The walls glowed with very pale, interchanging colors, blurring the world all around, as though standing inside a mirage.

I remember feeling very small and forgotten, as I often have in my life, but then someone came in, and bent to look me in the eyes, and remained like that for a long time, as though checking—searching. The eyes were blue, and the coat was black. He said nothing the whole time, he just looked, and I got the strangest feeling. A comforting rush in my belly, as if I was seen—as if I wasn't alone.

As if I was safe.

When the wall flashes again, this time it reads

Sabine LeRoux next to the number eleven.

Relieved the wait is over, I shake off the confusing memory and push up from my seat to exit through one of the side doors. Down the hall, behind another door, number eleven turns out to be a little room with two chairs and a desk. I take the chair facing the desk.

The furniture is the same shiny black as the floors, as though molded from it. The walls and the ceiling are all one giant moving picture, clouds floating across a pale sky; a screensaver playing on a loop.

I'm not kept waiting for long. The door swishes open, and I look up instinctively, just as a ghost enters the room—an apparition from the past— dressed in the same soft blue uniform as all the others.

At first, all I do is blink at her, convinced my eyes are playing tricks. *What is she doing here? Why did she come back?*

The blonde hair is shorter, cut straight and chin-length, exactly like mine. It's a popular hairstyle these days, the bluntness of it intentional, meant to embody order and correctness. The eyes have changed, too, like the green has faded, but then I suppose the cure does that.

I'm speechless for a moment, unsure how to react. I haven't seen Corinne in years. She left almost eight years ago now, to become a healer in one of the big city collectives, and that's the last time any of us saw Rory's big sister. All we'd ever received since were letters, stories of her new busy life.

In those letters, it always sounded like she never meant to come back.

And yet here she is.

Right away, I think: *this can't be good. She wouldn't come back for just any reason.*

Something has happened.

"Sabine." Her voice is barely marked with recognition, her face flickering with the faintest of polite smiles. "Good to see you. I'm here to do a few, quick tests."

I can't find my voice and she doesn't wait for me to. She sits and produces various pieces of medical equipment from the desk. Some are the usual ones; others are completely foreign.

She works fast, barely meeting my eyes, moving efficiently through the motions, as though functioning on autopilot. She takes my blood sample with a prick of my finger, checks my reflexes and my temperature, flashes a device in front of my eyes while I attempt not to blink.

One of the devices scans my brain activity, which then appears on the smart-wall. I peek at it from the corner of my eye, wondering if you can see it. The cure. Does it show up on scans? Does it look the same way it feels, like a piece of my mind has been taken out? I search the projected image, but I can't tell if anything is different.

Corinne relaxes in her chair and studies me, her minty eyes poking holes into my composure. Eyes identical to Rory's.

I want to ask a million questions but don't know how to start—don't even know if I should. Are questions allowed?

"You're not sick physically." Corinne's voice is flat and even. "But it's your mental health I'm concerned about. How are you feeling?"

It's a simple question and yet it terrifies me. "Fine," I lie.

She produces a tablet of smart-glass from one of the drawers and quickly types in my response. She doesn't put it on privacy mode, so I can see every word through the glass. Each jab of her fingertips on the touchscreen is like a nail being hammered into a coffin and my pulse quickens.

This feels like the most important test of all.

"Please direct your attention to the wall and tell me what you see."

I do as she says, swiveling in my chair. "I don't see anything."

"Very funny. Just give it a second to start."

The first thing that appears is an image of a

meadow. When she asks me how it makes me feel, I describe how the meadow looks.

"What's that?" She hasn't heard me. I'm speaking too softly again.

I dig deep, trying to locate my voice, trying to pull it to the surface. It resists, my throat tightening, and I push against the pain. "Peaceful," I try louder. "Sunny."

A smile flickers on her face for half a second. We continue, repeating the same process over a series of images, and I try my best to focus but it's hard.

Corinne would know if something has happened to Rory. It might even be the reason she's returned.

It has to be.

"You're distracted," Corinne notes. "Pay attention."

The next image is of two bicycles leaning against a white picket fence.

"Rory," I blurt without thinking. "This one reminds me of my childhood with Rory."

My words seem to hang in the air after I've said them, and I feel a shrinking feeling inside, sensing I've made a grave mistake. When the image of the bicycles abruptly vanishes, followed by the wall turning blank, it takes me another full second to realize what's happened.

I turn to face her, and Corinne has her finger on the power button. She shut it down.

She doesn't say anything for long seconds, and she doesn't look at me. Her face is human-shaped, but the humanity has been wiped from it, probably long ago. There's only the sound of our breathing—hers is calm, mine is coming out in short, uneven spurts.

Finally, she snaps into action. She taps one final thing into her tablet, and then quickly closes my file before I can read what she wrote.

In a rush, she's at my side.

My voice comes out smaller than ever. "I failed, didn't I?"

Her face doesn't move an inch. "Yes, but you can't tell anyone. You don't know what they might do to you, or to me, or to your stepfather if they find out. We could all be guilty by association."

Guilty by association. Those words stick in my brain, and I blink at her in shock. "What—"

She reaches out and clutches my hand, squeezes hard, speaking in a fast, hushed tone of voice that doesn't match her expression. "Promise me you won't tell anyone. I'll make the necessary arrangements, so it looks like you passed, but then you have to walk out of here and pretend for me, okay? If you don't, we'll both be in trouble."

I stare at her speechlessly.

"Sabine, do you understand?"

"I understand," I say, even though I don't. Right now, I understand almost nothing.

"Good. Now promise me. Promise you'll do everything you can to stop them from finding out about this."

I've become trapped by her gaze, by her words. Distantly, I know this is about Rory. She's warning me for a reason. Something really has happened— something always does to the people I care about.

I want to know more—I *need* to know—and I open my mouth to ask, but she shushes me with a sharp wave of her hand.

"That's all I can say for now. There isn't time. But you have to promise, Sabine."

I barely manage to choke out the promise. Satisfied, she helps me out of my chair and towards the door, a firm hand pressed into my back.

"Remember what I've said," she whispers—her voice crawling into my skull, where it will undoubtedly haunt me for days—just before sending me out into the world, armed with nothing but dangerous secrets and unanswered questions.

7

Outside the clinic, the sun is blinding, casting a sharp edge to every glass and steel surface. I squint on my way to the car. It waits, shiny and black next to the stark white of the sidewalk. My peacekeeper stands by the door in his long coat, the sun behind him, a black hole of a shadow where his face should be.

That's how we've started referring to them. *My* peacekeeper, *your* peacekeeper. It sounds ridiculous, like we own them, when it's actually the opposite. They are the shepherds, and we are the sheep. But it would sound even more ridiculous to call him by his name. I know what it is. I've heard it on the wind, whispered like a bad omen—like it's the name of bad luck itself.

Alexei Rolfe.

As I approach the car, he looks scarier than ever, knowing what I know now.

I am uncured. Cursed, as always.

He opens the door for me in some backwards gesture of false respect, and with Corinne's words echoing freshly in my ears, I'm struck with a surge of paranoia. Without thinking it through, I march past him and round the car to the other side, eager to keep my distance.

If he's displeased by this, he doesn't show it.

Once we're seated, the smart-car starts with a gentle sigh, and as we drive away, I keep my eyes trained ahead, focused on making my expression neutral. With every exhale, I imagine I'm emptying myself, letting the humanity drain out.

I don't look, but I can feel the peacekeeper making a study of me with those accusatory eyes.

"It went well?" His tone suggests it didn't.

I straighten my back. "Yes, thank you."

"What did the healer say?"

"She said everything was good."

"Did she say you can go back to work?"

"She didn't mention it."

He exhales. "I'll consult the report when we get home."

He sounds so convinced there's something wrong, I'm worried Corinne's plan has already failed, but either way, I have to try.

Because I'm so focused on sitting still and keeping my eyes forward, I don't immediately notice the commotion outside the car. Motion flickers briefly in my peripherals, a flash of something unrecognizable, but before I've had the chance to realize what's happening my peacekeeper has already yelled for the car to stop.

We screech to a halt, our seatbelts slamming us into our seats. My mind lurches, trying to catch up —trying to understand. In the blink of an eye, the peacekeeper is unbuckled and out the door, while all I can do is helplessly watch the scene unfolding.

Details click into focus slowly, one at a time, like an old movie reel. Each frame sliding together to form a moving picture.

A man is running. Not a normal run, not the kind for exercise or for chasing your dog down the street. This is a life-or-death kind of running, arms and legs pumping as fast as they can, face red.

In the near distance, someone is shouting threats.

I realize they're coming from the clinic, and the moving picture all clicks into place: *The runner is trying to escape.*

My peacekeeper's hand goes straight for his holster, and in the next instant, he's lifted the paralyzer gun, shiny black metal. When it goes off, it sounds like what lightning must feel like, and my body jolts as though I'm the one suffering the impact, a scream lodging itself in my throat. I force it back with sheer force of will.

The runner doesn't realize what's happened right away. There's a brief and sickening delay in reaction, a breath of stillness between the shot and what comes after. Then his legs collapse onto themselves and he hits the pavement, writhing violently, a full-body convulsion with eyes rolling back into his skull.

He's landed directly in my line of vision, in front of the open car door, and that's when I recognize him. It's Toma.

Peacekeepers rush the scene, black coats lining up like a wall. One of them has a nose that's gushing blood, the kind you get from an elbow to the face.

I remember the way Toma had looked in the waiting room, like a man on the precipice of something dangerous. In my mind, I think, *of course*. This must be the price he pays for making eye contact with the cursed girl. I must be responsible somehow, a walking doomsday. I always have been.

I'm thankful no one is paying attention to me right that second, because I can feel the shock frozen on my face and the blood draining from my cheeks. Corinne's efforts would have been wasted.

In the air, there's a smell like something burned.

In contrast to the horrifying scene, my peacekeeper seems wholly composed. He straightens to his full height and runs a hand over his hair, smoothing back the strands that have fallen out of place. The gesture reveals a scar on his forehead. It's wide, like a deep gash that should have been stitched but wasn't. Was it really there this whole time? I can't believe I ever missed it.

A cured person would never avoid medical treatment—it would be too careless, too irrational—so it must have happened before. *Before the cure.*

The discovery is a shocking one. A part of me thought peacekeepers must have been born cured. As if they popped right out, pure and clean, but the evidence is there on his face: He was human, once.

My stomach twists.

Two of the peacekeepers lift Toma by his arms and drag him away before the scene can attract too much attention. In the near distance, a lone figure stands in the street, watching with vacant interest. I'm not sure what's worse, seeing peacekeepers in action or seeing citizens not care what they do.

"Thank you, Alexei," one of the peacekeepers is saying, and there's a tinge of something in their voice—respect? admiration? "Excellent as always."

My peacekeeper grants them a swift nod before folding his long limbs back into the car, and every molecule in my body prickles with revulsion at his close proximity.

As soon as the car door shuts, time rushes forward again.

As we drive away, I resist the urge to glance behind at Toma, most likely being dragged back to the clinic. What happens to him now? One can only guess. The same thing that will probably happen to me, if I'm not careful. I may have just witnessed my own future.

I pray I don't look as horrified as I still feel. My insides are knotted up, painful and tight, and I can sense the peacekeeper aiming his focus at me, checking for cracks and for flaws.

"What are they going to do to him?" I ask, my voice going weak in the way that it does.

He still manages to hear me. "You shouldn't ask so many questions, Sabine."

I realize my mistake and clamp my mouth shut.

8

Returning to work is a strange sort of relief. A distraction, if nothing else, after being stuck at home, trapped and helpless in the face of my stepfather and our peacekeeper.

Even more strange is the fact that being around my stepfather has become more unbearable than being around the peacekeeper. My stepfather may still be here in body, drifting through the house quietly as always, but now a sort of fog surrounds him, muting the world all around.

Seeing him like this is a lot harder than I expected, and I'm glad we won't be seeing too much of each other, with both of us working long hours.

The glass towers of downtown Reye greet me with their impassive faces, as though they've forgotten me already in the short weeks since we last saw each other. They feel like giant strangers looming from above, judging me silently.

I hadn't noticed before how eerie they look, all identical and carefully placed in a measured line-up. An entire street of glass cathedrals and white concrete.

My company's logo sits atop one such building. A giant black orb with tiny veins running through it, like a marble—or an eye staring at you, unblinking. Just one word—*Onyx*—glows from its center in bold lettering.

Not many people get jobs at Onyx. We're responsible for all the security systems in Reye, and only the best are assigned to their entry training program.

When I got my letter of acceptance, I thought of my mother. Would she have been proud of me? It's impossible to know. She had been mentally absent for a long time. Years. Her name was scribbled on a waiting list for the cure, tucked away in some obscure digital folder, never to be seen or heard of again.

If only she were here to see this, all of us being forced to receive the cure. I wonder what she'd think.

As I exit the car, my feet remember the way. I follow the crowd into the belly of the glass beast, as though on autopilot. At the gates, I half expect the building to reject my access card, but the light flashes green and the door swishes open. I ride the elevator up to one of the middle floors, all the while rehearsing in my head how to act cured.

This is a building with eyes everywhere, security cameras fitted into corners.

I'm dreading the attention of my return, but walking into the office, I might as well be a decoration on the wall. No one is surprised to see me, no one comments on the fact I've been gone.

No one is themselves anymore.

I fight off a sudden chill as I make my way to my desk near the back of the room. There's a sweater still hanging off my chair, forgotten many weeks ago, and I quickly put it on, wrapping it tightly.

Maybe I'm unaccustomed to the air conditioning after being away, or maybe it's something else.

The office still looks the same—grey carpeting and black steel walls, lamps of blue light and spherical work desks—but an unfamiliarity clings to it. Perhaps it's because there are others still missing, stations sitting vacant and abandoned, and no one bothers to mention them.

Or perhaps it's because, two places down from mine, Rory's workstation is hauntingly empty. I glance over, as though she might materialize and give me one of her mischievous smiles.

We signed up for this job after graduation, went through training together, spent our lunch breaks sitting side-by-side.

And now she's inexplicably gone, and I have to pretend not to notice.

I look away and face my smart-desk, activating the touch screen monitor by pressing a series of taps into the corner—a personalized entry code. The system responds to my touch, the smart-glass flickering to life, and our company logo appears, the same giant black orb that's on the outside of the building.

At least the system appears to remember who I am, which is more than I can say for my stone-faced coworkers, each of them frozen in their seats with their eyes glued to their screens.

I try to copy them and focus on the workload for the day, my muscles immediately aching from the effort of sitting so straight. My screen fills with tasks, a long spreadsheet of breaches in security that need to be investigated, random house checks that need to be implemented.

How ironic, that I'm the one overseeing these things. I'm not even sure what Corinne wrote in her report after I saw her, but whatever it was, it worked. I am being trusted, for now.

Although that doesn't mean I'm not being watched. We all are. Not just from the peace-keepers, but from our friends and our neighbors. Anyone.

Out of the corner of my eye, I catch a flash of movement. The girl sitting at the desk in front of Rory's drops a stylus. It slips right out her fingers and rolls towards the edge of the smart-desk. When it clatters to the floor, she bends to reach for it, which is when she catches me watching.

She's a tiny little thing, hasn't been with us long. Big dark eyes and a head of shiny, tight curls. Her name's Josie, I think.

Our eyes lock.

Has something as simple as dropping a stylus become dangerous? Neither of us seems to know. We're both caught in a moment of hesitation, debating what's just happened. Maybe nothing.

But then again, maybe not.

Josie's dark eyes are wide. Is she afraid? Is she like me? If she is, she tries to mask it. Her expression visibly shuts down, her jaw clenching, and suddenly I wonder if I'm the one at fault here. She snatches the stylus quickly off the floor and resumes her work.

I straighten in my seat again and pretend I saw nothing—did nothing—while another chill creeps up and down my arms. It feels like the air conditioning is blasting me intentionally, a vent positioned just right overhead, marking me as its target.

I've become too fragile for this new world. A world where everything is cold and hard.

I shrink deeper into my sweater, stuffing my free hand into one of the pockets to warm it up.

I freeze when my fingers crumple around a piece of paper tucked into the lining of the pocket. I don't remember leaving anything there, and as I pull the paper out and unfold it, I quickly realize why.

The handwriting isn't mine.

I have to read it a couple times, trying to make sense of what I'm seeing. There's only six words on the page, but I don't quite believe my eyes.

"We know. Find Rory. Or else."

At first, I almost laugh. Or else? Who says such a thing?

In fact, the longer I look at it, the more ridiculous the note seems. Like a children's game. A joke. A prank.

Except my heart beats fast, like it doesn't think it's funny at all.

I instinctively sneak a quick glance around the room, wondering who might have left it. Someone here? The sweater has been hanging off this chair for weeks. Anyone might have left it.

But then why would they say "we know"?

My mind latches onto another possibility: *Is this a test?*

If it is, I decide the best course of action would be not to react, so I carefully refold the note and replace it into the pocket.

△△△

"You've returned," Ayn, our supervisor, says when we see each other in the lunchroom. She's the first person to comment on it since I arrived.

"I was out for a while, after my curing."

"I know," she says. "Weeks."

I still have to fight the urge to wince, every time I hear that word. Weeks. It's hard to believe it was that long.

On the far-right wall, the meal trays are slid out on a conveyor belt through a hole in the wall, each tray filled with the exact required food groups for optimal health. You have the option of a hot meal or a cold. We never see the cooks, except sometimes in the mornings, when we're all showing up for work.

Ayn grabs a plate from the available meal trays and starts crossing the tile floor towards me. The rest of the lunchroom consists of long white tables with glossy surfaces, and chairs set up to sit face-to-face. There are limitless options, the place is empty, but Ayn takes the seat across from me, where Rory should be.

I try not to visibly stiffen in my chair.

She doesn't appear to notice my discomfort. In fact, she seems remarkably unchanged compared to some of the others, like the cure barely disrupted a thing—like it agrees with her. She was always the unexpressive type, with unreflective eyes and a flat pink line for a mouth.

It's only when she blinks that there's the tell-tale mark on her eyelid. The marks go away after a time, mine was gone once I woke up from my own curing, so she couldn't have been cured that long ago.

"Happens to some of us," she continues our conversation. "Not everyone wakes up right away. Smith is still down. Jude only woke up yesterday."

It doesn't escape my notice she hasn't mentioned the most important person of all. I contemplate not mentioning her either, but the note still weighs heavy in my pocket. Could Ayn be the one who left it? That doesn't seem likely. As a supervisor, she's never built close relationships with the staff, as a gesture of professionalism.

I decide to take a chance anyway.

"And Rory," I add softly.

Ayn looks up, eyes narrowing on my face. They were always kind of vacant, weren't they? Like she'd always looked a bit cured, even before. "No. Rory woke up right away."

I struggle to keep my face still. "Then where is she?"

Ayn stares, her face so blank she might be looking at a wall. "I suppose you wouldn't know, since you've been out. She had to go in for a second time."

A second curing.

My fist closes around my fork. "And?"

"No news yet." She resumes eating, like it's not important.

"No news at all?"

"None," she says between bites, with such painful indifference I feel myself prickling, a mixture of bitterness and resentment.

I push the food around my plate, wondering how I'm supposed to eat now my appetite has vanished. I wait for Ayn to leave before dumping the rest into the bin. Do cured people waste food? I have no idea. I'm beginning to feel like we're becoming two completely different species—the cured and the uncured.

And the sick. We can't forget the sick. Even though they might be extinct soon.

I'm reminded of this very real possibility when I return to my desk. Just as I'm sitting down, two peacekeepers cut around the corner into the office, boots thundering across the carpeted floors. We all look up and watch in silent suspense. For a second, I'm convinced they're here for me and my cheeks grow hot.

They stop in front of Josie's desk instead. I should have known, but I'm still surprised. I study the back of her skull as she looks up at them, her hands frozen at her touchscreen. The peacekeepers bend to speak in hushed voices, so I can't make out what's being said, but I can see her shaking her head, the ringlets bouncing. Back and forth, back and forth, desperation clinging to her shoulders.

Should I say something—do something? I feel helpless, just sitting here, watching.

Before I know it, they've forced her out of her chair and out the door. We only hear one word echoing clearly across the office, in the split second before she disappears for good. A loud and resounding, "*No!*"

The sound of it shudders through me, and my eyes snap back to my screen.

As I resume my work, only six words remain on my mind: *We know. Find Rory. Or else.*

Yes, the sickness may very well become extinct soon, marched out by peacekeepers just like that in the midst of an otherwise ordinary afternoon, never to be seen or heard of again.

And I might be next.

9

Over the course of the next few weeks, it's a struggle to adjust to this new life full of order and secrets. Every day exactly the same, a mind-numbing routine, with me growing more and more desperate not to draw any unwanted attention to myself.

After the day I found the note, I flushed it down the toilet, but the words still haunt me every day and I have the sensation that I'm running out of time somehow. Only I don't know how much time, or what I'm supposed to do.

At the end of each workday, our peacekeeper waits for me outside, parked among the cars idling at the curb, all of them lined up like a funeral procession. Bodies exit the buildings in near terrifying unison, a march of sorts. The end of the workday march. All of us at the same time, like clockwork. *Tick, tick, tick.*

As usual, I do my best to blend in, to appear as cured as the rest. It feels like I'm getting away with it most times. At least, that's what I tell myself, and I'm hoping if I believe it hard enough it'll become true.

Other times, I feel like I'm hanging by threads, likely to snap at any moment.

On that day, a day no different from any other, something inside me inexplicably unravels, my marionette strings falling away like ribbons.

I spot her up ahead amidst the crowd, and my feet come to a halt halfway down the concrete steps.

Even from the back, I recognize her. The blonde hair, the exact shape of the skull. When she turns her head briefly, scanning the line-up of cars, I catch sight of her profile. The delicate bone structure, the rosy complexion.

It's her. It's Rory.

I'm not aware of anything around me as I start to move. The people fade to faceless, shapeless creatures as I bump shoulders with them, pushing through in my eagerness to catch her. I don't stop to question why or how she came to be here. I don't stop to worry what it'll be like, seeing her cured.

All I care about is not letting her slip away.

She's headed towards one of the parked cars, her long legs eating up the ground fast, and panic rises in my throat.

"Watch it," someone says as I shove passed

them. I don't even pause to look at who it was, my eyes locked on Rory.

The door to the car opens, ready to swallow her up and take her away, and all at once, the blood rushes down to my feet and my ears are ringing. This is quickly turning into a nightmare.

Deciding to throw caution to the wind, I call out, "Wait!"

The girl stops, turns to look. For one long precious second, she looks exactly like Rory. Minty eyes and everything.

Then I blink, and she's gone.

The blonde hair isn't as light, the eyes aren't even green. In fact, she looks so different, it's a mystery how I could have mistaken her for Rory at all.

Wishful thinking can be a dangerous thing.

The stranger gazes at me with mild, polite confusion. "Do I know you?"

I'm too stunned to say anything right away. I wanted her to be Rory so badly, my heart clenches like a fist inside my ribcage.

"Sorry," I eventually manage. "I thought you were someone else."

The stranger blinks twice, before slowly climbing into the car and shutting the door, the illusion of Rory disappearing behind black-tinted windows.

I watch the car drive away, my heart still clinging to a phantom hope.

Then a shadow appears at my side, and the air changes temperature. A chill gathers at the base of my spine, crawling up like a spider, and a glimpse over my shoulder confirms it's a peacekeeper, her face frozen in an emotionless mask.

"Are you alright, citizen?" she asks in a robotic voice, and every click of her eyelids is like a computer analyzing, sifting through data.

I don't know what to say. It feels pointless to deny anything.

"I think you'd better come with me." The words are a direct order.

Her hand moves to the back of my neck, latching like a claw, steering me away from the curb. My feet comply before I've even had the time to process what is happening. I find myself in motion, although towards what, I am unsure. These feet cannot possibly be mine, headed towards a cliff— a point of no return.

Something inside me collapses.

This is it. I have been caught.

Although I'm aware the consequences awaiting me are heavy, I feel strangely detached. Like this couldn't be happening to me, it must be happening to someone else.

I resign myself to my fate, until another hand reaches out from seemingly nowhere and grabs my wrist, wrenching me to a stop. I shudder like a puppet at the end of its ropes, but who is the puppeteer? Suddenly, I am trapped between two unstoppable forces—two dark, menacing coats.

Alexei looms from above with all his impressive height, his blue eyes sharp as glass, and I can't tell if he's my rescuer or the real threat.

"Go back to the car," he commands in a low voice. "Now."

The other peacekeeper stares, a watered-down shock marking her face. "Peacekeeper, I witnessed this citizen—"

He cuts her off smoothly. "She was doing as I had instructed."

As usual, he does not yell, does not raise his voice. He is soft-spoken in that way of his which is always somehow worse, rendering the other peacekeeper speechless.

Her claw of a hand slips off my neck, releasing me. A gush of cool air hits where my skin is damp with nervousness.

After another moment, she recovers and nods her head once. "I see. My apologies."

She takes a step back, and I realize I've been holding my breath. Air tunnels back into my lungs with alarming speed, making my head spin, and I struggle to remain upright as we separate into op-posite directions, Alexei steering me away with an uncharacteristic urgency.

When I'm safely strapped into my seat and Al-exei instructs the car to take us home, I can scarcely believe it. I lean my head back against the plush headrest and stare up into the skylight, watching the clouds blurring overhead.

That's a bit how I feel right now. Like a cloud. Like I might be losing my mind.

10

Alexei doesn't say a word as we drive home. Even when the house comes into view, a perfect white cube of concrete against the green slope of the yard, he continues to say nothing.

The car parks in the garage, and we wordlessly enter the house. Alexei shrugs out of his black coat and slips it onto a hook in the entryway. For some reason, the gesture seems symbolic of something, although I can't say what.

The coat doesn't look altogether harmless, hanging there. Like there's something alive about it. I shudder at the thought, and I'm considering making my escape to my room, eager to hide away, when Alexei finally breaks his silence.

"Just a moment, Sabine," he says calmly.

I grit my teeth. I wish he would just shout. I wish all these cured people would quit being so stifled.

Reluctantly, I stay put and face him.

He approaches, until we're standing very close. He's still wearing the peacekeeper boots, and each stomp to the floor reminds me of what he is: A threat.

But then why did he rescue me back there? Why bring me home safe, as though I've done nothing wrong?

"I was hoping to have a moment to speak with you," he says in a low voice.

My pulse hammers in my ears.

He lowers his voice even further. "You need to hide it better than this, Sabine."

It takes me too long to understand what he's saying, because my mind wants to reject it. Hide what? What am I hiding? My mind shifts from confused to defensive and back again, until I remember: I am hiding something. Something important.

"What you did back there," he continues, "it doesn't look good. You shouldn't draw so much attention to yourself, or else I'll have to report you."

I want to laugh, partly from disbelief, and partly from a rising hysteria bubbling in the pit of my stomach. "What are you saying?"

It's a stupid question, because of course I know. I picture Toma and Josie. I picture a paralyzer gun, and a group of black coats dragging me away, and after that there's a blank space for whatever comes next—the unknown thing that's happened to Rory, the very thing Corinne warned me about and tried to protect me from.

"I'm saying you need to be more careful."

I scramble to formulate a thought. "But why— why would you—"

"It's my job to protect you."

My eyes drop to the floor as my cheeks burn, a mixture of guilt and embarrassment, my hands curling into fists. I've let Corinne down, not to mention possibly put her in danger, and that thought alone makes me furious.

I'm angry with myself, of course, but it's easier to direct it at him, so I cut my voice extra sharp when I say, "So why don't you? Turn me in?"

I tilt my head up at him, but he barely blinks in the face of my dare.

"The risks are much higher, the second time they try to cure you. I've seen it go wrong. But you're not sick, Sabine. You're not a danger to anyone. If I thought you were, I would have brought you in already."

The words are painfully similar to Corinne's, and I feel myself shrink as he towers above me.

"Maybe the cure hasn't worked as well for you," he says, "but that doesn't make you dangerous."

I absorb those words, trying to make them fit

with my newfound reality. For the first time since we've met, my impression of the peacekeeper has become unfocused, confused. Something has changed, something has become misplaced.

The mask of authority dividing us has shifted slightly, just enough to reveal a little bit of his humanity.

I look up into the face of my enemy—the eyes are blue, blue, blue—and I wonder: Is this what my enemy looks like? Is he like me? Flesh and blood and water? Are we the same?

I can't decide if this is better or worse.

When I speak again, it isn't from a place of courage. Strangely enough, it's a feeling of defeat which motivates me to ask, "Can you do something for me, Alexei?"

He looks surprised, and it's the closest thing to a proper emotion I've seen on his face. Although I'm not sure which part is surprising to him. The fact I've dared ask for a favor? The fact I've addressed him by his real name? Maybe he didn't think I knew it.

"What is it you need?"

I take a deep breath. "I need to see Rory. I need to see her with my own eyes."

He immediately shakes his head. "Sometimes it's better, not knowing."

"But you know where she is, don't you? You

know what's happened?"

He hesitates, which is an answer on its own, even before he says the word. "Yes."

A rush of hope spreads through me. "Then I won't stop trying until I know the truth."

He holds my gaze. "You could get us both in trouble."

"Not if you arrange it."

I'm being too bold. I know I am. But I feel like I have nothing left to lose, and I'll hate myself if I don't try.

Find Rory, the note said. As if I wasn't already trying to do just that—as if that wasn't exactly what I'd wanted since the moment I woke up from my curing. I still don't know who wrote that note, but maybe when I see Rory, I'll find out.

"She might be dead," Alexei warns, and I can tell he doesn't say it to be cruel. He wants me to be prepared for the worst.

I lift my chin and pretend the possibility doesn't terrify me to my very core. "I *need* to know."

There's a long pause; too long. I'm sure he's about to refuse.

What he says is, "Okay. I'll figure something out."

11

The morning air is crisp when I leave the house. The sun is bright in the sky, and it feels like an insult. Today is not a happy today, the sun shouldn't be so bright.

My peacekeeper waits in the driveway, black coat standing tall. My stepfather is already at work; we have the rest of the morning.

Alexei holds the door open when I approach, and today I'm not afraid of him. I'm afraid of something else. A part of me knows I won't like what I find, but at the same time, it's eating away at me, the not knowing. I have to face this—I have to do this for her.

Which is why I climb into the car, instead of turning around and running back inside to hide beneath the covers of my bed.

The drive feels both long and slow, all the way to Rory's family home. We sit in silence, staring out the windows.

Alexei is the first to speak. "Why do you need to see her so badly?"

I turn my gaze in his direction and find him already looking, waiting. Embarrassed, my eyes return to the window. "Because I have to. She's my only friend."

"What?"

He hasn't heard me. My voice has gone small again, as it often does when I speak of things that are more personal—important. The more important, the quieter I get.

I repeat myself.

He hears me this time. "Why is she your only friend?"

"I don't exactly know how to explain it," I say, "but when I'm with her, I don't feel invisible."

He says nothing at first, and it takes him so long to respond, I fight the urge to check what his expression looks like, strangely afraid of what I might find. Or not find.

Finally, he says, "You're not invisible. I watch you all the time."

"Because it's your job."

"No," he says, "it's not that."

I want to ask him what he means, but we both fall silent, because we're pulling into the driveway now.

My stomach does somersaults. Suddenly it feels too fast, too soon. I'm not ready.

The house sits on the far end of the lawn, a cube of glass and steel. Smart-homes, they call these, the insides fully equipped with all the latest technology. Much fancier than ours, but a house shouldn't be smarter than its owner, my step-father used to say. Back when he had thoughts and opinions of his own.

"Please be careful," Alexei warns.

He sounds afraid I'll reveal my terrible *uncuredness*. As if it were a thing separate from myself, capable of escaping its confines, slipping out through the bars like a slithering snake.

I can feel that snake right now, coiling around my insides, and I dig deep for a bit of bravery—for those words from Rory herself which have become the voice in my head, reminding me to be strong.

Don't be a coward, Sabine.

Be like Rory.

I pause to reach out and touch the peacekeeper's hand. I'm almost surprised; his skin feels human. "Thank you, Alexei."

He doesn't react, and although it's strange, seeing these cured people and their non-reactions, I realize I don't mind. There's always a little flash of humanity behind his mask—the ghost in the shell—reminding me we might not be as different as I thought.

How did we end up on opposite sides of an invisible war? Why have I always thought of us as enemies? Today, he feels almost like a friend. At least, it's comforting to pretend he is. Although it's probably unwise, getting too comfortable around a peacekeeper.

He is the embodiment of authority and oppression, and perhaps by making friends with him, I am making friends with something else—like the construct of a tyrannical society I was born into. Perhaps it's wrong of me—a sort of betrayal. Am I an accomplice in my own oppression if I make friends with a peacekeeper?

No, I decide. I can't deny my own humanity. My ability to see him as a friend is a reflection of who I am, isn't it? It's important, I think, not to lose this piece of myself.

I can't let them take it.

I offer Alexei a smile, a silent promise I'll do my best in there, before I pop the door open and step outside the car. The gravel crunches beneath my shoes, and I wince each time, as if someone, somewhere will notice me and hear my inner thoughts, guess my secrets.

At the front door, I pause before ringing the doorbell, struck by nerves. Alexei has to reach over my shoulder to press the button.

We hear the robotic ring, followed by the beep of the door unlocking when we're permitted entry. It automatically swishes open with a gasp of air, and we step onto the entry mat and remove our shoes.

Rory's mother comes around the corner to greet us, her hair and clothes very neat, her face smooth. Angela knows who I am but doesn't show any other signs beyond basic recognition.

It catches me off-guard, and I attempt to stifle my reaction. I was close to Rory's family, once. I hadn't anticipated what seeing them cured might be like.

Alexei nudges me forward, a silent warning. I'm already slipping—he's already noticed.

Thankfully, Angela hasn't.

"Sabine," she greets me with a vacant smile, her dark eyes flat. Besides the blonde hair, she doesn't look very much like either of her daughters, something I always thought was a bit strange. She lacks the delicacy, the vibrancy which Rory embodied.

I often wondered where Rory got her magic, since her father didn't seem to have it either.

Angela leads the way to Rory's room, even though I know where it is. I've been here a million times—has she forgotten?

Our feet pad across the white carpets, and the house smells the same, triggering memories which come rushing at me. I'm helpless against them, until the door to the bedroom opens, and

I'm helpless against something much worse.

A healer is in the room, donning the soft blue uniform. There's a young woman on the bed, hooked up to a breathing tube and a monitor. Her blonde hair is splayed against the pillow, soft and feathery, and her minty eyes are hidden beneath eyelids criss-crossed with veins. Purple and blue. Deep shadows gather in the hollow of her cheeks, and in the crevices of her neck, which looks alarmingly skinny.

She barely looks like Rory at all. I don't believe it's her. My mind resists what it sees, instead searching for excuses. I have to stare for long minutes, forcing myself to accept what lies before me.

The air in the room feels beyond stifling.

"She's not showing signs of improvement," the healer says, and her voice is too loud, it feels disrespectful. Doesn't she see Rory is right there? She could hear. "We'll have to remove her life support, if she doesn't get better soon."

The words are a slap to the face. I recoil, backing straight into Alexei. He puts his hands on my shoulders to steady me.

Somehow, I remain upright. I keep my face even.

It's strange how the mind works, how difficult it is to understand something like this, even when you see it with your own eyes. I struggle to make the connection between this unconscious body before me and the vibrant life it once held.

So, this is what a second curing looks like. Something between death and sleeping. Something without peace. This is what will happen to me, if I'm exposed for what I really am.

I think of George, the one secret Rory never got to tell. A small and selfish part of me thinks I can have him to myself now, but just as quickly as the thought manifests itself, I banish it from existence.

George has and always will be hers, and I wouldn't have it any other way.

"You're welcome to come." Rory's mother touches my shoulder. "On the day we take away the life support. I know she would want you there."

The words cut straight through me, but instead of feeling something, the opposite happens. My insides freeze and turn numb.

"Of course," I say, and my voice sounds like it belongs to someone else. "I'll be here."

I don't know if I'll be able to keep that promise. I'm sure an excuse can be made, when the time comes. Either way, it doesn't matter, because Rory is already gone. That thing sleeping in her bed, it's not her. I'm sure she'd understand, if I chose not to watch her body meet its end.

The body doesn't make the person. Rory was so much more.

△△△

I manage to make it back outside, although I don't know how. The air feels cold and unkind. I've started to shake, which means I need to get out of sight quickly. I'm unraveling. I miss a step on the stairs and Alexei catches me just in time.

I press into him for support. He plays the part of protector now, and not just for pretend. All at once, he's become an ally in my tangled web of secrets. Maybe because it's easy to make friends with inanimate objects. Like a doll you dress up in the appropriate clothes—a suit of armor for a knight—a role to play.

"It's okay," he says, his voice both patient and urgent. "It's okay, you did it. But you need to get in the car now."

The remaining steps are a blur. I crawl onto the seat, and Alexei shuts the door. He climbs in from the other side and orders the car to take us home.

"We'll pretend this never happened," I say, looking out the window at Rory's house, watching it shrink in the distance as we drive off.

"Okay," he says.

I have no tears. I feel like there should be tears, but there aren't. My mind blinks in and out, trying to make sense of this. I can't remember what feelings are supposed to feel like.

"I don't know what I expected to find," I speak to the car—to anyone who'll listen.

Of course, Alexei is the only one here. He knows my secret, I remind myself. He knows I'm not cured, which means I don't have to be so careful around him. The idea thrills me. I want to dump all my feelings and non-feelings into his lap and see how he handles it. I want to challenge him with my uncuredness, like a game of dare. A dangerous one.

I laugh in the face of danger. I don't care anymore. Rory is gone. Everyone I care about leaves me.

The curse prevails.

"You were right to keep me away," I speak slowly, each word brought forward with physical effort.

"I'm sorry you had to see that," he says, "but I wanted you to understand the risks, to understand why it's important you hide being uncured, not just for the sake of yourself."

I nod. "You were right. I see that now. You were just trying to look after me."

Alexei barely moves, his face like stone. "I try."

"It's your job," I say.

He nods his head, the blond hair shiny like metal. Gold.

I'm jealous. I'm not made of gold, I'm made of nothingness. The nothing, it sinks beneath my skin, settling into the crevices of my existence. I am the invisible one—the forgettable one—the cursed one.

I am nothing now.

12

In the morning, I don't move. Alexei comes to my bedside. "If you don't go to work, it'll look bad," he says.

He wants me to be careful, but I can't listen to him right now. Careful is a language I no longer understand. Instead, there's a rushing in my head. My thoughts have become static.

He brings me soup and medicine. "It's just for show. We'll pretend you've got a cold. It should buy you a couple days."

I just stare at the wall. The whiteness and flatness of it. I wish I could be that: a wall. A solid instead of air. My body floats, my words are fumes.

Alexei leaves, but he keeps coming back. Every time I hear the door, I roll away and pull the covers over my head.

After three days of this, he insists I go to work. "I can't cover for you any longer."

Because I believe him—because I trust him, a concept that is entirely new and frightening, but I have no one left to trust—I get up. I take a shower. I get dressed. I move fast through the motions, relying on the speed to get me through.

At work, Rory's desk has been removed. It seems a bit drastic, to have it removed completely. They could have used it or hired someone new to replace her.

"How was it?" Alexei asks, later, during the drive home at the end of the day.

He's taken the habit of checking, as if I'm a ticking time bomb. I kind of feel like one.

"Fine," I say. I've been practicing that word, rehearsing it in my head, so I can get the tone of voice right. "They took away Rory's desk."

"I know. I asked them to."

I look at him. "How'd you manage that?"

"I asked if they had any spare desks they could donate to the curing efforts."

The words just hang there between us. Finally, I manage to say, "Thank you."

We say nothing else after that. I find talking exhausting, these days. I've become quieter. The quietness is something I'm good at, but I can't help wondering: Is this what it means to be sick? Is this what it was like for my mother, for my sister?

△△△

Being invisible used to be a curse. Now, it's a blessing, making it easy to hide in plain sight. I float from one day to the next, and I know there's something wrong. Something has become disconnected inside. But no one else notices, which seems ridiculous. How can they not see it?

Sometimes, I sit at my desk at work and think: what would happen if I just started screaming right now? If I just started to scream and never stopped? It's actually an effort, holding it back.

Is this what it was like for Sara? Did she feel like this all the time and that's why she took the pills?

I never understood the sickness. How could people give up on themselves? How could my mother give up on me and Sara? I still have pictures from when we were little. Mother would hold our hands, a twin on each side. Then our stepfather came into our lives, and we seem normal in the pictures, a complete family.

I used to stare at those pictures for hours, trying to make sense of what became of us.

Now, I feel like I know a little bit. I've tasted that darkness, and I'm starting to see how it blocks everything else out.

I keep waiting for Alexei to turn me in, I kind of hope he would, but he doesn't.

My stepfather is trickier. He definitely notices my behaviour, although he doesn't comment on it. We drift around each other like ships passing in the night, since we both work long hours and don't often see each other. It's always been this way between us, but it's worse now. Even when he's here, he's not the same.

The isolation is the worst part. Even Alexei, who is showing me mercy against all odds, doesn't fully understand what it means to be uncured. He listens and tries to help, but he can't know what it's like.

I feel like a freak. Like I'm the only one this has happened to.

Until I'm not.

13

It's raining that night. Colder than usual. Darker. My stepfather is working late at the library, Alexei has left to pick him up. From the living room window, I watch the car pull out of the driveway, the rear lights disappearing into the night.

Barely two minutes pass before I hear the knocking.

At first, I'm not sure it's real. Maybe a trick with the wind, a tree tapping a window, or the rain puttering loudly on the metal roof. Another knock, and that's when I realize it's coming from the back door, through the kitchen. I pad across the floor in my socks and peek around the corner, my heart stuttering.

The timing is too perfect. Whoever is out there has specifically waited for Alexei to leave.

Through the glass doors, I recognize the silhouette and my heart beats faster. *Why is he here, an hour passed curfew?*

I don't turn on the lights, afraid of being seen by

the neighbors. I grab the smart-glass tablet from the kitchen counter and disarm the house security system, before creeping closer, drawn to the forbidden. The glass door slides open too easily, considering all the rules being broken.

George stands tall, dressed in head to toe black, soaking wet from the rain. He ducks inside, and then towers above me, dripping onto my floor mat.

We assess each other, bearing witness to our crimes: Him, showing up here like this. Me, opening the door. It seems ridiculous that such simple things could become so dangerous.

Finally, he speaks, "I knew it."

I only stare at him in disbelief.

"I knew it, that day you chased me down the street, that you were one of us." He reaches for my hand, clasping it urgently. "I couldn't say anything, there were too many people around, but I knew. That's why I sent Josie with the note."

I struggle to keep up with what he's saying, too distracted by the feel of his hand in mine, big and warm and strong. He's gazing at me so intently, I feel breathless—weightless.

Until I come crashing back to reality.

It's wrong of me—how can I care about such a thing while Rory is dying in her bed at home?

I snatch my hand back. "How did you make

it here without getting caught? It's dangerous, showing up like this."

He doesn't listen to a word. "Sabine, there are others. Uncured people, like you and me. You can come meet them."

What he's saying should mean everything to me. This means I'm not alone.

Instead, what I say is, "I can't. Alexei will be back soon."

As soon as the words have left my mouth, I'm hit by a stab of guilt. Like I've betrayed him in some way.

George looks shocked—I've spoken the peace-keeper's name, a thing nobody does because it makes them seem like one of us—but he recovers, apparently choosing to overlook my slip-up.

"Not right now. Later tonight, we're having a meeting." He grabs the tablet that's still sitting within reach. "You should be able to access your home security on this thing. Do you know how to erase any history of activity?"

I nod. I work for Onyx. I know how to tamper with security systems.

"As long as you're careful, you should be fine." He puts the tablet back, and reaches into his pocket, producing a wrinkled piece of paper with an address and a time scrawled on it. "Meet me here."

He forces the paper into my hand, and I hold onto it, mostly out of confusion, staring at the letters and numbers as though trying to decipher their meaning. They seem so innocent on their own like this, incapable of being dangerous.

The handwriting is exactly like the first note.

George steps back into the rain, a smile splitting his handsome face. "I'll see you later then?"

He looks so hopeful; my heart nearly shatters. "Okay."

There's no time to regret it. In the next instance, he's gone again.

△△△

Nightfall makes everything worse. Noises are louder, the dark is deeper. I went to bed dressed to go out, wearing my darkest layers of clothing, and I hid a pair of shoes in the closet.

I carry the shoes into the kitchen. I'm about to disarm the security system, I've got the tablet in my hands, all smooth glass beneath my fingertips, when behind me, there's a sound. I suck in a sharp breath, and at first, I think I'm being paranoid, but then I hear it again.

A pair of tired feet slide across the floors, socks on hardwood, coming this way.

I abandon the tablet and back away quickly,

tucking myself against a wall, out of sight. I clutch the shoes tightly to my chest, and tiptoe carefully towards the pantry, so I'm not out in plain view.

Is he really coming in here? Am I really that unlucky?

I am.

My stepfather comes around the corner, yawning hugely, eyes closed.

There's a sliver of space between the pantry and the fridge, and I squeeze myself in at the last second, holding my breath. In the dark, my stepfather shuffles to the other end of the kitchen, his back to me. I press a hand over my mouth, to muffle the sound of my breathing.

If he catches me here, I don't know what I'll do or how I'll ever explain it.

He has an empty drinking glass in his hand, and he stops at the sink, yawning again. That loud, old-man yawn. Like a public announcement for how tired he is. Then there's the tap water running. It just keeps on running, for too long it seems like.

I notice his shoulders drooping, and strands of hair shining silver even in the dark, and I'm shocked by how old he looks. When did that happen? We've never had a close relationship, and I always blamed him for that—blamed him for choosing Sara to be his favorite. I always assumed he regretted being stuck with me, in the end. Stuck with the cursed girl. But maybe that was unfair. Maybe, if I tried a little harder, I could take care of him the way he's taken care of me. He looks like he needs it.

Finally, the tap stops running, and I feel a pang of sadness watching him retreat to his room with his glass of water, all alone. What would he do, if he ever found out I wasn't cured? I'd hate to disappoint him—hate to burden him even more.

I wait until I hear the sound of his bedroom door, down the hall, shutting softly. Then I exhale a breath of relief.

It's a long time before I leave my hiding spot—before I know it's safe. I remain frozen, squished between fridge and pantry, my head buzzing with doubts. Should I just go back to my room, slide back under the covers? It would be so much easier.

Then I think of George, and before I know it, the tablet is in my hands again and I'm disarming the security system. I'll delete the evidence later, when I return.

I pull the hood of my sweater over my head as I reach the door. The rain outside has turned to a mist, coating everything. I put on the shoes, making sure to be quiet about it. In my pocket, I have the slip of paper. If I leave now, I should make it, as long as I don't get caught.

I slide the door open and closed as gently as I can, and then that's it. The easy part is over.

I feel a shift in the universe the moment my foot leaves the back porch and touches the grass. Quickly, I cross people's backyards, keeping my eyes peeled for any patrolling peacekeepers. I feel like a criminal—a sneak. Even though I'm hardly doing anything outrageous.

I find myself holding my breath most of the way, until I find the right house. It sits on a corner, behind a big hedge. The outside is blue steel, and I realize I'm starting to feel torn about this color. What does it really represent? The sky, the healer's outfits, *Alexei's eyes?*

Despite being such an offensive shade, the house looks small and unthreatening, the windows all dark, like everyone inside is asleep. I worry I've made a mistake. What if it's the wrong house? What if I've misinterpreted the handwriting on the page? Or, even worse, what if this is a trap?

I only walk up to the back door because I figure it's too late. I've already done this, I've come here. If they mean to catch me in the act, they will. I'm too far from home now.

I knock three times, as instructed on the paper.

The door opens a crack, and a voice rises softly from within. "Name?"

"Sabine LeRoux," I whisper.

The door opens, and nothing but darkness

awaits. I'm careful about where to step, not wanting to bump into anything. The door shuts the second I'm in, and a shadow of a person stands to the side. They gesture to a flight of stairs that descend into the basement.

All over again, I'm terrified that this is a horrible, horrible trap. But I go down anyway.

14

There's another door at the bottom of the stairs, only I don't knock this time. I'm not sure if I'm supposed to, but I don't.

As soon as I step inside, I get the impression I've done the wrong thing. A staggering number of eyes turn to glare, stabbing me with accusations. A handful of people stand huddled around a table with a single light bulb hanging from the ceiling above, casting jagged shadows across every surface.

It feels like an interrogation room. Cold, clean, sterile.

A young man with long hair—dark blonde, almost long enough to touch his shoulders—sits at the head of the table, smoking a cigarette. His eyes are thin as slits and they brush over every inch of me. The cigarette is the most shocking piece, because they're banned. They're the sort of thing sick people smuggle amongst themselves —a health hazard, an illogical habit—the sort of thing that could get you arrested on the spot.

I freeze, unsure of what to do. I'm an intruder, and I've never felt less invisible in my life. My skin crawls. I desperately scan the faces for a familiar one, but there are none, and I suddenly regret coming here with every fiber of my being.

What was I thinking?

At the same time that I ask myself the question, I know the answer. I was thinking of George. That's why I've come. All I cared about was that George had asked me, George had held my hand, *George would be here.*

"I'm sorry," I say to the room, only because I don't know what else to do.

The apology isn't welcomed. They shoot daggers with their eyes.

"Is your name on the list?" someone asks.

I nod, unable to find my voice. This makes me seem more suspicious, apparently. One person frowns, another crosses their arms over their chest. I'm being evaluated, studied, picked apart. They are considering whether or not I should be permitted entry into their secret world of rebels. Perhaps they will ask me to take a test, to prove my worthiness by doing something dangerous and insane. I dread finding out.

Finally, I manage to say something that isn't completely stupid. "George asked me to come."

The explanation is met with better reactions.

The room appears to relax, although they still don't seem too impressed, like I've alarmed them needlessly.

"Is he here?" I ask.

"Not yet," a brunette girl says, sidling closer now I've proven not to be a threat. "He should be here soon, though."

I'm guided to a chair and instructed to sit, while the others remain standing. The sitting makes me feel like I'm being punished—like I'm a child being put in a corner. They are active participants, and I am not.

I'm otherwise forgotten as conversations are resumed, most of which I don't understand the context. Something about supplies, a shopping list, but things that don't make sense. Fertilizer, fruit, copper wire.

All the while, the long-haired man gazes at me from the corner of his eye. He blows smoke up into the air, aiming it in my direction, which feels vaguely insulting.

I'm terribly relieved when George finally makes an appearance. He parts the crowd with his tall frame and walks straight at me. His hand lands on my shoulder and he squeezes, as though we are old friends.

It's funny how times of crisis will bring people together, uniting against a common enemy. Before this, George had barely noticed my existence.

It makes me feel worse, not better, that he's being so friendly now. As if the past never happened—as if years of being overlooked can be smoothed over with a single gesture of kindness.

"This is Sabine," he says to everyone. "She and I share a common friend. One that is very important to both of us."

I ache at the reminder that we've both loved Rory—that we've both lost her. She connects us in some invisible way and perhaps always will.

"A friend who, at this very moment, is in a coma due to a failed second curing." George's voice booms, like always, only now it means something more. He holds the attention of everyone in the room, ensuring my acceptance into the group.

His introduction is met with nods of approval, and the first step of my initiation is complete. It makes my head spin to know I'm being so easily woven into a group I'm not even sure I want to be a part of.

George takes my hand and holds it again, like he did back at my house. He looks so happy I'm here, it almost makes up for everything else. Almost.

"This is my friend, Markai," he introduces me to the long-haired man. "He's the one who's brought us all together."

"Nice to meet you," I say.

"Likewise," Markai snaps back.

I nearly grimace, but I manage not to. I've gotten better at keeping my emotions below the surface.

Markai smiles, as if he knows. "You're doing it."

The other conversations in the room fade, and now the attention is on me again.

"Doing what?" I ask, trying to ignore all the eyes in the room.

Markai leans forward, elbows on the table, so I can really smell the smoke on his breath. I try not to choke.

"You're holding back," he says. "You're so used to it, you don't even notice. But you're keeping your emotions in check, making sure no one knows that you're *feeling*."

He pops the cigarette back between his lips, takes a long drag, and waits to see what I'll say. He's got such a smug look on his face, I want to smack it away.

There's something about him that makes me feel off—like he's not someone I can trust.

Despite this, he's right. I'm so used to holding back, I don't even know how to stop. Plus, it's been so long since I've seen uncured people, I've forgotten what it's like.

Nobody here is hiding. Everyone is showing

their emotions. The room is full with it—tension, anxiety, excitement. It feels almost offensive, having all these emotions thrown in your face.

Without meaning to, I squeeze George's hand tighter. I'm already leaning on him—turning to him for support. It makes me hate myself sometimes, how weak he makes me. He doesn't even have to try.

Maybe one day, I'll stop loving him. But right now, he squeezes back, and it's like every part of me comes alive.

Markai laughs without restraint, head thrown back and everything, and I feel myself shrink. He wipes a non-existent tear from the corner of his eye. "The new ones are always so adorable."

George smiles, rubbing the back of my hand with his thumb. "Just relax, Sabine. You can be real with us."

I try. Because George asks me to, I try.

"Stop tormenting the new girl," the brunette from earlier pipes up. I wish someone would tell me her name, but no one does. "Let's get back to the task at hand."

She plants her palms on the table. The light bulb hangs above, casting a spotlight on her features. She seems like a severe sort of person. Everything about her is hard, from the straight hair scraped back against her skull to the crisp lines of her clothes. I get the feeling that, if you grabbed a fist-ful of her shirt, it would crunch like paper.

This is someone who doesn't have time to waste—someone who commands attention.

She produces a map from under the table, which she flattens for everyone to see. Our small collective is displayed neatly in bright colors. It's not often you see printouts like these, so it's interesting to look at.

She points to a covered bridge. The one outside the library, where my stepfather works. "We'll plant it here. All we need is a time, so we don't risk hurting anyone innocent."

She marks the spot with a bright red marker. The room becomes very still, everyone waits. This is a test—a shock tactic. *No time to waste*, the brunette seems to say, her chin pointed at me.

I don't move. I barely breathe. All at once, the shopping list makes sense. I know what they're planning. I can feel the eyes on me from all directions, but I can't look away from the X marking the map. Red and splotchy, like a blood stain.

George rubs little soothing circles onto the back of my hand, but now it hurts almost, grating against my skin like sand. I swallow with difficulty but manage to remain calm. I've become good at that, the pretending.

Markai starts laughing again. That offensive,

machine-gun laughter that I already hate. "Well, she hasn't gotten up and run out of the room."

At that moment, I look up at the many faces surrounding me, and a sound bubbles up my throat. Of all things, it's a laugh. I can't hold it back. It's a laugh of nerves, if I'm honest, but it shifts the mood instantly.

Everyone joins, as though encouraged. They've misunderstood.

Meanwhile, I don't share their relief. Not one bit. I'm rigid in my chair, my mind swarming with escape plans. I want out, but I don't know how. I don't know how to fix this. There's just too much attention, all directed straight at me, and I'm suffocating under the weight of it.

George looks proud, his handsome face beaming, dimples showing. He looks younger than I've seen in years. "I told you guys she was one of us."

The words seal my fate. The others all nod.

The brunette is the only one who doesn't appear convinced. She leans closer. I stare back, pinned in place by her scrutiny.

There's only one question on my mind. "Who's the target?"

She smiles, abruptly, a flash of white teeth. She's misinterpreted my intentions, too. She produces an object from somewhere—was it beneath the table? Was it in her pocket? I missed something, like a glitch in time, because suddenly there's a pen in the center of the table, shiny stainless steel. Harmless looking.

I stare at the thing, waiting for an explanation, because I suspect it isn't harmless at all.

"It's a tracker," the brunette says, picking it back up to examine it in the light. She turns it this way and that. "When you click the top, it activates." She clicks it a few times, to demonstrate. "It could be easily slipped into a pocket, undetected, giving us the exact location of the person we need."

In a rush, she cuts across the room and thrusts it at me, her chin pointed confidently. I put my palm out, like an automatic reaction. The pen feels normal, and I slowly close my fist around it.

It's a simple gesture, accepting a pen when it is offered to you. And yet I can sense the significance of it.

I am one of them now. Part of the club.

No, I scream internally. *I don't want this. I didn't ask for this.* But it's too late, no one can hear me.

There's a beat of silence that follows. Markai smokes, still looking smug. George is still clutching my other hand, but I want him to stop. It's like he senses how badly I want to rip away from him, so he holds even tighter.

They all wait for me to clue in. There's a reason I was chosen—a reason I was brought here.

They needed me for something, and George volunteered to get the job done. I can see it playing out in my head like a movie, all the little moments adding up to this one. This is why George is being so nice, why he's suddenly acting like we're the best of friends. It wasn't because Rory connected us or because I chased him down the street. It wasn't even because I work for Onyx.

My heart sinks, dropping into my stomach. I think I might be sick.

"The target is Alexei."

15

The brunette looks manic, now I've said his name. "He's the perfect one, don't you see? He's the most respected, the one with the worst reputation. It's the only way to send a clear message, with the least amount of bloodshed."

She sounds so sure of herself, convinced her plan is a work of art.

It's like the day I visited Rory all over again. My mind shuts down and my insides feel numb. I gaze blindly into the eyes of the brunette girl, and I realize they're the same color as mine. Pale gray. The only difference is that hers are full of life, while mine have always seemed dull somehow. Her eyes are the color of storms, and mine are the color of ghosts—the color of dust. Just like the rest of me. Something that is here but isn't, something forgotten.

It makes me feel less than, simply being in her presence. It was the same with my sister and with Rory, like flying too close to the sun.

It suddenly frustrates me so much my entire

body clenches like a fist.

"No."

The word pops out, so perfect and dense, that everyone is surprised. Even me. My voice has never sounded like that before.

"No," I say again, thrilled by the sound of it. "I won't hurt anyone."

A moment of tension follows. It crackles in the air, lingering like the cigarette smoke, choking us just the same. It's the scent of oppression, that nicotine. Addictive, like a trap.

George speaks first. He bends his tall frame to be more at my eye level.

"I get it, Sabine," he says. "Of course, we don't want to hurt anyone either. It's sad, really, that things have come to this. But doing nothing, sometimes, is just as bad as anything else."

I stare at him while he speaks. Earlier tonight, minutes ago even, I couldn't resist him. Now his words mean nothing to me.

The brunette jumps in next. "Think of everything that peacekeeper has done. He shot a man in the street, right here in town. He's ripped people out of their homes, locked them away from their families."

She's desperate, I can smell it on her. She wants this plan so bad and she needs me for it. An inside man to help set the stage, someone who knows where Alexei will be and when.

George leans in real close, whispers into my ear. "Think of Rory."

My entire body breaks out in chills. *Think of Rory.*

"Think of what they've done to her. You went to see for yourself, didn't you? Just as I instructed in the note? I wanted you to see the truth. She's in a coma, Sabine. She's dying, right now, as we speak. *Because of them.*"

I blink at him, stunned by his audacity to use her as a way of manipulating me. George blinks back, silently pleading, oblivious to my sudden, vicious hatred. It materializes so fast, it leaves me breathless.

"Are you going to let them get away with that?" He says it like a dare.

Is this supposed to be the "or else" part of his note? Find Rory, or else let them get away with it?

This is all about revenge for him, I realize, and I start to shake. I know I am, but I can't help it. The tracker pen rattles in my fist.

Are they going to let me walk out of here? They've already told me too much. I know their plan. Outside the library, on the bridge.

All they need me to do is drop the tracker in Alexei's coat pocket.

But I won't do it. I keep my mouth firmly shut, lips pressed into a flat line.

George sighs, like he's disappointed, but the brunette is undeterred. She's not giving up yet.

"Give her some time to think. We've dumped a lot on her tonight. I'm sure she's tired," she says, then she looks right at me. "You hold onto that pen. I know you'll do the right thing."

George stands to his full height, looking hopeful again. He smiles like he's trying to alleviate the tension. "You're right, Cee. I'm sure this has been a lot to take in."

Finally, I have a name for her. *Cee.* It doesn't suit her. It's too short, too sweet.

I say nothing, worried they'll change their minds. This is my one chance to get out of here.

"I'll walk you home," George says to me, still with that tone of voice. I can see it now, how hard he's trying.

I simply nod, not trusting my vocal cords. My throat is painfully tight.

△△△

Outside, the rain has stopped and the air is damp and fresh. I hadn't realized how stifling it had been in that room, with all those people staring, and the cigarette smoke.

George walks quietly at my side, a small smile playing on the corner of his mouth. I bet he thinks that went well. He thinks he got away with it. He's still holding my hand and I feel like a prisoner being escorted home. I feel like I did in the beginning with Alexei.

Now Alexei has become something else to me—he represents freedom instead of imprisonment. He's the one person I've been able to rely on and be honest with. It makes no sense, and yet it's the truth. People aren't who they seem to be, not at first, and I don't know who to trust anymore. My mind is knotted up, trying to make all the puzzle pieces fit.

When we reach my backdoor, George pulls me to a stop. I don't have time to realize what he's doing before he's leaned down and kissed me, softly at first and then not softly at all.

He's trying to manipulate me, and that's the awful moment I realize: he knows. Perhaps he's always known how I feel about him. While his mouth moves over mine, I flush hot with shame. This whole time he'd known, and he hadn't done anything about it. This whole time he'd known I wanted him, and yet he hadn't wanted me back.

I would willingly lose to Rory a thousand times over, but it still hurts.

The kiss is nothing like when I'd seen him with her. This one is too intense, forced. It feels like blackmail, and it has the opposite effect than he'd intended. I feel repulsed and angry. I've never wanted him less.

Our mouths part with an inelegant pop, a release of suction.

"You know joining us is the right thing to do." He pushes his forehead against mine, his hands on either side of my face, trapping me.

"I'll think about it," I say, because I just want him to let me go. I just want to go inside and forget about this whole night.

"Don't let them brainwash you. Remember how they targeted you, how they assigned you one of the worst peacekeepers, how they made you one of the first citizens to be cured."

I shiver at his words, wondering if he knows something else that I don't.

"Think of Rory," he adds at the end, his voice dropping lower.

But I am, I want to say. *I am thinking of Rory. All the time. Every second of every day. And Rory would never choose this. She wouldn't be a part of something this ugly.*

I don't say any of this, though. Because I realize I pity him. He wants revenge, someone to blame, because he's sick with grief. Does that make him a bad person?

Does it make me one, for not wanting the same

things?

Finally, George moves away, releasing me, and smiles. The smile remains perfectly frozen on his face when he says, "I don't think I need to emphasize that we expect complete silence from you."

This, without a doubt, is a thinly veiled threat.

I don't know what to do or think. I nod, hoping that'll be enough. He nods back, and then he stands there, watching me creep back inside my house.

I remove my shoes to avoid making any sound, and go to the counter and pick up the tablet. I access the settings and erase all history of tonight, wishing I could do the same with my thoughts. When I arm the security system, I wish I could do that, too. Arm myself against the world and lock myself away.

The whole while, I feel George's eyes boring into my back, through the glass door. Whether he's actually there or not, I feel his eyes. I feel all of their eyes.

They'll be watching me from now on.

My feet drag the whole way to my room; I've never felt so exhausted. The events of the night are clinging to me, the feel of George's poisonous kiss still burning on my lips.

When I open the door, Alexei is sitting on the edge of the mattress, waiting.

16

Alexei stares at the floor. The small lamp on the night table casts a warm and comforting glow across the room. I'm so relieved, I don't care he's here to confront me. I want to tell him everything. The words are right there, poised on the tip of my tongue. Alexei is the one person I can be honest with. That's his purpose in my life right now, and I want to tell him the truth.

I open my mouth, ready to unload everything, only to promptly slam it shut again. Something holds me back, a thought pops into my head.

What will happen to George, if I tell Alexei everything right now? He'll probably be arrested. Can I betray him like that? What would Rory think?

I couldn't live with myself, knowing I betrayed George—knowing Rory would hate me for it.

The tracker pen feels like it's burning a hole in my pocket as I stand in the middle of the room, torn.

No, I decide. *I won't betray them.*

But I won't help them, either.

Alexei doesn't notice my internal struggling. He lifts his head slowly, and I can tell he's disappointed, even if his face doesn't quite show it. "Should I ask where you were?"

"It doesn't matter. It's not going to happen again." My voice sounds as tired as I feel.

He frowns. "Are you okay?"

"No. Not tonight. Tomorrow, maybe."

I'm not sure why, but he doesn't ask any more questions. He helps me into bed, flattens down the covers. Taking care of me, like he has been, because it's his job.

He turns off the light.

I sit up. "Alexei?"

He stops, looks at me.

George's words from earlier are still swirling around my head, punctuating every thought. "Can I ask you something? Will you tell me the truth?"

He waits for me to continue.

"Is there a reason I was one of the first citizens to be cured?"

He doesn't say what I expect him to. "How much do you know about your father?"

"Almost nothing," I admit. "Mother died with that secret."

"Then I won't tell you."

It's not what I wanted to hear. "You won't?"

"It's my job to look after you, remember?"

"I remember," I say.

He stands there a moment, unsure of something. Then he approaches again, sits next to me on the bed, his back to the headboard and his legs stretched out. It doesn't escape my notice he's positioned himself perfectly between me and the door.

Has he placed himself there on purpose? Is he making a statement, making sure I don't sneak out again?

"Go to sleep," he says, and he reaches out to touch my hair, tucking a strand behind my ear.

The gesture might be intimate, with someone else, but it's alright because Alexei is cured, and everything is good and safe with a cured person. They would never do anything wrong.

Except neglect to turn you in to the authorities when they should.

That thought bounces around in my head for a bit, but I drift off to sleep before anything else can follow.

△△△

By morning, everything seems normal. I go to work. Alexei drives me there and back. We don't say a word to each other. I don't know what to talk about, after last night. I want to convince myself it was all just a terrible dream.

But then Alexei leaves in the late afternoon to pick up my stepfather from the library, and I hear a knock at the back door. It's very faint, and yet it seems to echo through the whole house.

They must have been watching the house again, waiting for me to be alone. It's George. I know it is.

He's probably here to ask why I haven't activated the tracker pen yet.

I don't answer the door. I sit in the living room, rigid on the couch, looking out at the road, waiting for the car to return and make everything safe again.

I hear the knocking once more, a little harder this time, but it stops after that. He must have given up.

In my bedroom, under the mattress where I put it, the tracker pen waits in silence. A promise the rebels will be back, knocking again, demanding things from me. Outside, the sun is setting, painting everything in shades of gold. Like the world is on fire.

Somewhere in the distance, sirens are screaming, as if they know.

△△△

My stepfather stays up late working on some documents at the kitchen counter. After he goes to bed, it doesn't take long before Alexei's footsteps come down the hall, soft and careful, all the way to my door. He doesn't knock. He just walks in, and I've got the light on, a book in my lap, as though I've been waiting.

He looks relieved, like he wanted to make sure I hadn't snuck out. He shuts the door, and I wonder if he intends to stay and watch over me like he did last night.

"I told you," I say. "It won't happen again."

He crosses the room to sit by me on the mattress, sticking his fingers under his collar to loosen the buttons. He looks like my very own guardian, sitting there, the body of a man encased in that uniform, so it hardly looks human anymore. When I catch a glimpse of it, my eyes instinctively trace the scar on his forehead, this tiniest of proofs that he was uncured once.

I consider telling him everything. George was here again this afternoon; the rebels must want me to be part of their plans. They're watching the house, and they're being patient for now, but who knows for how long? I can't ignore them forever. They might find a way to put their plans into action without my help.

But how can I tell Alexei any of this? They said they expect complete silence, I can still hear George's threat in the back of my mind. They'll know if I talked, and then who knows what might happen to either of us?

I'm trapped in a game of lies and secrets.

"Be careful," is all I decide to say.

Alexei looks at me. "You're the one I'm worried about."

"Maybe we both need to be careful."

He sighs and stretches out at my side, a mirror image of last night. He looks tired. Sometimes I forget we're the same species. He doesn't always seem like it. At least, not all the way. He looks like only half a person, dressed and decorated like a machine. That ominous black coat which hangs in the entryway like a flag of death.

It's in rare moments like these, when he closes his eyes and I can see the deep lines marking his face, that he looks like he's carried too many burdens.

I study his features, the straight line of the nose, the strength he holds in his chin. "You work too hard."

"You make my job difficult."

"Sorry. I'll try not to, from now on."

His mouth twitches, and if I didn't know any better, I'd say he wants to laugh. Cured people don't laugh outright, but they do this, they smile halfway.

I flip the pages of my book and listen to him breathing, and suddenly my bedroom feels like another world—a place separate from the society in which we live.

17

Mornings are strange. Alexei rises early, long before me, to slip out of my room and back to his own, so my stepfather never catches us.

When I see Alexei again at breakfast, he's dressed in a clean uniform, his face freshly shaved, and he won't meet my eye. It makes me feel guilty of something, even though we haven't done anything wrong. We've only broken some small rules, and I've been trying not to think too much about what that means. It could mean nothing, after all.

"I'm working a half day," my stepfather tells me that morning. "We can have supper together. I was thinking chicken."

It's a rare occurrence these days, having supper together. All he does is work. I suppose that's what they want. They're making machines of us, wiping away our emotions, so we can work ourselves to the bone.

At least it's Friday. I'm looking forward to a weekend of rest. Your soul gets weary, after so many hours of pretending to be cured.

After driving my stepfather in for his early shift, Alexei returns within a half hour, and I say nothing during my ride to work. There's a silence between us. In the night we can talk, but we're quiet during the day. The daylight exposes our imperfections—our sins. It reminds us to be careful.

The second the car pulls up to the curb, I feel like I'm being watched. I'm not sure what it is that alerts me, something in the air that day. Stepping out, I glance back at Alexei sitting in the front seat, as though he can somehow offer me reassurance.

He smiles a little. Halfway.

I force myself to keep walking, quickly mounting the stairs of the Onyx building, while the others around me are oblivious to my panic.

There aren't as many black coats around today. One by one, the peacekeepers seem to be vanishing. Not all at once, but a slow trickle, barely noticeable but still there. Now that most people have been cured, we don't need so many of them.

It should be a source of relief, but today it makes me nervous. I feel exposed, without as many peacekeepers around to protect us.

Someone bumps into me from behind, mumbles an apology. I feel out of place, walking in a crowd of cured people like this, but today is worse somehow. My skin prickles under the cool sun of the morning and my eyes dart everywhere, trying to find the source. *Who is watching*?

The question is stupid, because of course I know. Someone from the other night—Markai? Cee?

I search the faces around me, looking for those grey eyes or the long locks of Markai, but I don't spot anyone I recognize.

It doesn't matter. Someone. One of them.

There's relief once I make it through the revolving doors into the air-conditioned building. I've done this march so many times, it's easy to move through the crowd of workers, my body on autopilot. This place is always packed in the mornings, everyone coming in all at once, overloading the elevators. I feel better once I'm at my desk, staring at my workload for the day. The routine is familiar, comforting.

I get started on a task right away, eager to shed my paranoia.

It isn't until lunch rolls around that things start to fall into place. There's a familiar face in the lunchroom, seated at one of the far tables. My heart stops. She's a tall girl with a short black bob and an upturned nose, as though she's always looking down on you with her big Bambi eyes.

Was she there this morning? Did my subconscious pick up on it?

She was definitely there the other night, at the meeting, although I've never seen her in this building before.

I grab a tray from the conveyor belt and immediately cross the room to her table. I slam the tray down, scrape the chair back. Her big eyes harden, like she doesn't appreciate my imprudence.

"What do you want?" I ask in a low voice, since there's no one seated close enough to hear.

"It's my first day," she says, and she sounds calm. She's perfected her act of being cured.

I'm too frustrated to be careful. "I don't want a part in this."

"It's going to happen either way." Her expression never matches her words. "Your stepfather is working a half day."

I frown at this. Why does that matter?

It takes me too long to catch on. My mind clicks slowly, going over her words one by one, as though trying to decipher a foreign language. She blinks at me dully, but there's an undercurrent. Like she knows something I don't, like she finds it funny.

Then the horror sets in: they're done waiting. They didn't need me to plant the tracker pen, after all.

The realization hits me in jolts, my mind and

body uncooperative with each other. My pulse spikes, but my thoughts scatter, jumping between denial and panic. I search the wall for the clock.

Her words still hang there between us: *Your stepfather is working a half day.*

Alexei will be leaving the house any minute.

I don't think. I jerk out of my seat, and the girl looks shocked for a second, before she has the chance to smother her reaction. A quick flash of humanity.

I don't care if they arrest me. In a matter of seconds, I'm out the room and down the hall, headed towards the elevators. I don't stop to explain myself to anyone, I just go, my shoes padding the floors as fast as possible.

I press the elevator button a dozen times, willing it to hurry. I can hear voices coming around the corner, getting closer, ready to catch me in the act.

The elevator doors slide open with a ding, just in time, and I throw myself in.

Downstairs, the security gates won't budge when I pass my access card over the reader. I'm leaving at the wrong time, the system knows I'm not supposed to. It beeps at me, as though frustrated, flashing red.

I don't have time to lose. I cut towards the emergency exit and push straight through. The alarm blares, but I don't let that stop me. I take off at a dead run across the expanse of white concrete, burning hot from the midday sun beneath my shoes.

The roads are eerily deserted outside. They've got the whole collective on a strict schedule, like clockwork, easy for them to monitor and control. The people going in and out of work like machines on a timer.

I knew this already, of course, but it's different seeing it during midday. A ghost town.

Perfect. No one around to witness what I'm about to do.

I aim myself for home and run with everything I have. I'm expecting to get caught—expecting a peacekeeper to materialize and tackle me to the ground at any moment, like that day I'd seen Toma trying to escape—the day I'd seen Alexei shoot him with the paralyzer.

I can already imagine what a paralyzer would feel like, biting into my nerves and frying my senses into nothing, until I'm flopping like a dying fish on the side of the road.

But there's no peacekeeper in sight. They're not patrolling the area like they used to, in the beginning.

Instead, of all things, it's a slab in the sidewalk that sends me crashing to the asphalt, my hands getting smashed against rocks when I reach out to catch myself. The breath is momentarily knocked from my lungs, and my pulse thunders in my ears, like distant echoes of the emergency alarm, chasing me.

Disbelief smashes into my thoughts. *What am I doing?*

I come face to face with my decisions, all of them lining up in my head, amounting to this moment. I can't believe I'm really doing this. This has to be the scariest thing I've ever done, risking everything for a peacekeeper, as though someone small and helpless like me could actually make a difference.

The afternoon breeze wafts over me, smelling of oranges and lemons. Just like school, just like the curing clinic. It doesn't make sense here, though.

Until I realize: Am I remembering something? Has the impact of my fall knocked something loose inside—a memory dredged up from deep within?

Jagged images flash before my eyes. It takes me a moment to recognize they're from the day of my curing, then I see it all clearly: The thin layer of cloud overhead, the dusty light. And there's that same memory I'd glimpsed once before, blurry around the edges. It slips into focus this time, and suddenly I can recall exiting the procedure room and being left to wait by myself.

Someone had come in, hadn't they? They'd put their hand on the side of my face, trying to get me to look at them.

How are you feeling?

The voice was Alexei's.

Did he ask those words?

He did. I know he did.

Scared, I'd said. It was the only word I could think of, and yet it was also the only one appropriate. Somehow, through the thick fog wrapping around my brain, I had been able to say the right thing for once in my life.

I feel so scared.

Don't worry, he'd said. *As long as I'm here, I'll keep you safe.*

With skinned knees and bloody palms, I push up from the sidewalk in a blur of determination and adrenaline, ignoring the way my knees throb, the way my ankles and lungs ache from running.

I launch myself back into motion. I have to make it in time.

When my house finally comes into view, rising in the near distance—a white square, a finish line —the garage door is shut tight, so there's no way of knowing if Alexei is home.

I'm panting hard, nearly breathless, when I

make it through the front door. I check the entry-way for his coat and boots, but neither of them are here, and the hope drains from me all at once —like I've just plummeted from a great height and been pulled to a sudden stop by a harness.

That quick snap against gravity, the body shud-dering at the end of the wire.

Denial clings to me, a refusal to accept defeat. Or maybe it's just the shock. I really thought he'd be here. I'm not even sure why I was so certain he would be—so certain I could save him. I try not to picture his body, lifeless in a ditch, as I float through the house, my feet mindlessly carrying me.

I check the living room, the kitchen.

"Alexei?" I ask each of the rooms, as though call-ing his name will somehow conjure him into the empty spaces I find.

He could have left a long time ago; he could be anywhere else in the collective. I don't even know what the peacekeepers do during the day, and I wish I'd thought to ask, just once. My mind tries to fill in the blanks, to imagine what a peacekeeper's life must be like, but I can't even think of any-thing.

"Alex—"

"What are you doing here?"

The voice is so unexpected, I'm momentarily

frozen. It came from behind me, soft and neutral, but it moves through the space between us and lands on me like a shout.

I turn. Alexei is standing in the hallway, already encased in his black coat and boots. His gaze catches on the blood trickling down my legs and lingers there a moment, before cutting back to my face.

When I open my mouth to explain, no words come out, my mind stalled between panic and relief.

"You can't be here right now." He's mad, I think. I've never seen him mad, but that's what it looks like. He immediately moves towards the front door, closer to it than I am at this point. "I have to pick up your stepfather. If I'm late, they'll suspect —"

I watch his hand land on the doorknob, and horror shoots through me. I know I have to stop this, but it's happening too fast. Either that, or I'm moving extra slowly.

The fear is instant and it blocks out everything else. I move without thinking, crossing the distance between us in a few fast strides. I touch him, and he's like stone beneath my hands, but I don't let go—I can't let him walk out that door.

What I do next, I tell myself I do to distract him —to make him stay. I tell myself that's the only reason.

But the truth is, maybe I do it because I want to.

I act quickly. There isn't time for anything else. I hold him in place, my fist tight around the front of his coat, and stand on tiptoes. The doing it part is strangely easy—strangely simple. As though I might have done this many times before. Alexei doesn't try to stop me. Perhaps he doesn't understand, a momentary confusion. I take advantage of it.

How far would someone go to save another's life? This hardly seems extravagant.

I kiss him like George kissed Rory, like I'm asking a question. A question only he knows the answer to.

I kiss him, and that's all.

He doesn't move, he just lets me, and there's a brief breath of stillness where I'm just kissing him and nothing else exists.

It isn't until it's over that I fully realize what I've done. When I release him, Alexei is glaring.

The embarrassment is fast and hot behind the panic from a moment ago, and I instinctively recoil. What was I thinking? There's a simple answer to that, which is that I wasn't. We've been too comfortable around each other and I've gotten confused. I've forgotten—I've forgotten that cured people don't feel, not like I do.

I've never been more afraid of Alexei than

in this moment, and something Rory once said, something I overheard in the labyrinth just before George kissed her, comes to mind: *I have the most awful feeling.*

I hadn't understood, back then, but now I think I do.

"Sabine," Alexei speaks finally, a warning.

He sounds like he pities me, like I'm something fragile that needs to be handled with care. My stomach twists with self-disgust, and my eyes drop to the floor in a weak attempt to conceal my true feelings.

The coats and the boots are stacked against the walls, hanging from hooks, bearing witness to my embarrassment. There is nowhere to hide.

"I have to go," he says, more softly this time. "If I'm late, it'll look bad. You being here is bad enough."

His pity is too much, and angry words spill out, almost of their own accord. "Is that all you care about? Do cured people care about nothing at all?"

I'm hoping an argument will distract him. I don't expect his response in the least.

"I'm not cured," he says.

18

He says it calmly, almost apologetically. I'm not cured. I look up and stare at him for long seconds, not understanding.

"How can I be?" he says. "A cured person would never have helped you like I did."

I don't believe it, at first. "But you—you act just like them."

"So do you. So does anyone like us—anyone who has to. I used to think it worked for me, but I've come to realize it didn't."

I wonder what made him realize he isn't cured. I wonder if it's me.

"You're not making any sens—"

"I have to go." He's really scared now. For both of us, I realize. "Don't you see what this could do? Why did you even come here?"

I don't know how to begin answering that. There's too much to say, not enough time.

He turns towards the door again. This time, he

doesn't make it outside.

We feel it when the explosives go off, even at this distance. The ground shudders like in an earthquake and all the lights in the house blink on and off. We catch ourselves on the walls, something falls off a shelf in the next room, we hear it shattering into pieces.

There's a beat of silence before the electricity clicks on again. The microwave beeps, the fridge hums.

I practically collapse from the relief. *It's over.*

Alexei whips towards me. His face shifts through a quick succession of emotions—he's panicked and confused, he feels betrayed and he's accusing me.

He turns and throws the door open, stepping outside. I follow, and we seek the horizon for signs.

A part of me didn't think they'd go through with it, but the evidence is here before my eyes. The smoke is a deep black, rising into the sky above the trees in the near distance. I know their target was the bridge, but I wouldn't be surprised if the building itself suffered damages.

"You knew," Alexei says, and it's not a question.

"I didn't know what to do. I'm sorry."

In the next instance, there's an alarm, ringing clear across the collective. Not the usual kind, like a fire or a security alarm. This is a state of emergency. The collective is equipped to defend itself. Mandatory evacuations will start downtown, people will be forced to return home. I have a feeling I won't need an excuse for my absence from work this afternoon. One problem solved, only to be replaced by another.

There isn't time to go into details, and Alexei starts pushing me back. "Go inside. I'll be back later."

I don't want to let him go. I try to reach but I grab nothing but air. He's already gone, there's no other choice.

Something inside me shrinks and I retreat to the safety of the house.

ΔΔΔ

After he's gone, I go to the bathroom and wrap my knees in bandages, then I change into a pair of pants to hide the evidence.

All the while, my mind replays the events of the day.

Did I really run here like this—skin my knees bloody—kiss a peacekeeper? Did I really save someone, instead of cursing them?

Today, I wasn't forgettable. I wasn't hidden behind my sister's ghost. Today, there was something interesting about me, the individual.

When I look in the mirror, the one hanging above the sink, I hardly recognize the face looking back. I get the impression I'm meeting myself for the first time, and perhaps that's true, in some way. Perhaps I have been invisible to myself, like I'd forgotten who I was over the years.

I'm not sure I had entirely realized, until this moment, how much I've lacked an identity of my own—how much time I've wasted, being contented living as other people's shadows. Now, all at once, like two images eclipsing each other, an identity superimposes itself onto my reflection.

Who am I?

I'm the kind of girl who isn't afraid to take risks. A girl who cannot be controlled, manipulated, or cured. *The kind of girl who falls in love with peacekeepers.*

△△△

My stepfather returns, alone. I meet him at the door and help him out of his coat.

"You're not hurt?"

"No," he says, and he actually sounds rattled for a cured person. "They sent you guys home, too?"

I nod, a small lie. "Where's our peacekeeper?"

"He had to stay there. They need all the help

they can get."

That makes sense, although I don't like it. We settle in the living room to wait, unsure of what to do with our time. My stepfather seems normal enough, but he also doesn't seem altogether calm.

I have to fight hard not to fidget. I could chew my nails clean off, I'm so nervous.

"Do you want to talk about it?" I ask.

"There was an explosion."

"But was anyone hurt?"

"No. It was just the bridge. A couple windows blew out, but that's it. They had to put planks over the river, to get us back across."

I listen while keeping my eyes on the window, hoping to see the car.

My stepfather rises from his chair. "I suppose we should eat something."

It's a bit early, but I don't argue and follow him into the kitchen. We cook something fast and eat standing over the counter. My appetite isn't strong, so I have to force the food down.

I figure I'll need the strength to get me through tonight, since I don't expect to rest until Alexei returns.

While we eat, we watch the news for updates, not that they're broadcasting any. They keep playing news coverage from other sectors, other collectives. Nothing about us.

Maybe they're embarrassed. Someone has gotten the best of them. Several someones. I can picture all their faces, standing around that table in the basement, the light bulb hanging overhead. Cee with her stormy eyes and her determination. Markai with his cigarette, poisoning us all slowly. The girl with the black hair I met today at work, the others, *George*.

This isn't as simple as the protests in the streets we had in the beginning, the incidents we saw reported each day on our television screens. They'd expected all of that, they knew there would be pushback during the early days of the new law.

Those days were violent enough, but this is worse. An act of terror.

That's why they aren't broadcasting it. They probably don't want to cause widespread panic. It would mean admitting the cures aren't working like they should—it would mean exposing their weak spot.

We watch the screen, the man reporting onsite at a bride market in another collective. In Reye, our bride markets don't get much news coverage, but in the bigger collectives, it's a thing. The festivals are huge, thousands of people crowded in one place.

It reminds me of Rory, and that time we snuck into the bride market together, and how I caught her with George in the labyrinth.

It seems ridiculous to be watching festivals, when there's a war waging in our streets.

I turn the TV off.

19

It's late by the time Alexei returns. He stands at the foot of his bed and waits for an explanation.

The best I come up with is, "I fell asleep. Sorry."

It doesn't explain why I've come to his room in the first place, but he used to do it, so why can't I? Nightfall is the only time we can really talk.

Tonight, he says nothing. He quietly removes his watch and unbuttons the collar of his shirt, his face marked with deep lines.

I sit up and fold my legs, feeling shy. He turns on the bedside lamp and then sits at the foot of the mattress, as far from me as possible, staring at the floor.

We're uncomfortable with each other now. His revelation has ruined things.

Nothing is safe anymore. Neither of us is cured.

"Are you alright?" I ask.

"No." A twitch of the mouth. I can't tell if it's

supposed to be a smile or a grimace. "Not tonight. Tomorrow, maybe."

He's using my old words back at me.

I find a loose thread in the bedding and pick at it. Since he won't look at me, I won't look at him. "Don't you want to know who did this?"

He sighs. "It's better if you don't tell me."

"Why not?"

"You shouldn't be too involved," he says. "You're already too involved."

It sounds like he's mostly saying it to himself.

"They might already be looking for me," I say. "I left work early to get here. I set off the fire alarm. They're going to see it on the cams."

"I'll take care of it."

"Okay."

He looks uncomfortable, and I desperately want to fix this sudden distance between us, but I don't know how.

"What happens next?" I ask, and I feel sad when I say it. He hasn't even answered the question yet, but already I feel sad.

He directs his words at the floorboards. "They're sending me away."

I'm not surprised. It's like I knew.

"Do they know the attack was meant for you?"

He shakes his head. "No one realized I was late picking up your stepfather—no one clued in I was supposed to be on that bridge when the explosion happened."

"Then why are they sending you away?"

"Because I'm one of the best," he says. He means one of the worst, although it depends from which angle you're looking. "They need someone they can trust to start the process in the next collective."

The process. Those words hitch in my mind. Is that what they call it? Invading and uprooting our lives, it's all a simple protocol to them.

There's a brief moment of silence while we both sit there in the glow of the lamp. I trace his profile with my eyes, willing him to look at me, but he never does.

Finally, I ask the important question, the one that's weighing on my mind. "When do you leave?"

There's a pause—a sigh. He sounds tired, and not in the usual way. "In the morning."

ΔΔΔ

From my bedroom window, I strain to see the car outside. It pulls up to the curb and idles softly in the dark. It doesn't seem the least bit apologetic for coming. Less than a minute later, Alexei's figure appears in his black coat, cutting a dark shadow on the front lawn. He strides down the foot path, never looking back. A single bag goes into the backseat with him. The door shuts.

I watch the car disappear, a tightness coiling my chest. Can it really be that easy? Can a person exit your life just like that? One moment they're here, the next they're gone, and the screen fades to black—the curtain falls.

A darkness settles over me, like a cloud shifting into place overhead. It's long minutes before I manage to walk away from the window.

By that afternoon, a new peacekeeper shows up. It happens exactly like it did when Alexei first arrived. My stepfather and I are both standing at the door, ready to greet him.

My stepfather even says the same thing. "I'll show you the spare room."

The peacekeeper nods. This one has dark hair and squinty eyes that are too close together, and he's not as tall, not as threatening. Maybe they're easing up on us a bit.

Or maybe there's no one else available.

He follows my stepfather through the house, towards the spare room. It's already been cleaned, someone came by to do it earlier.

After he sees the room, he comes back out to

speak to me, pointing those little eyes. "I'm afraid I have a few questions for you."

He leads me into the kitchen, and we sit at opposite ends of the table. The peacekeeper places a recording device on the table, and I watch the little red blinking dot, my throat tightening.

"This is just a precaution," the peacekeeper says. "Due to the recent incident."

I nod and sit very still.

He takes a tablet out and reads from the document on the screen. "The day of the incident, the reports show you were at work until the evacuation."

Alexei must have taken care of that part, like he said he would. I nod again.

"Then what did you do?"

"I came home and waited for my stepfather."

He looks at me, then back at the screen. "You were at home with him for the rest of the day?"

"Yes."

He types something. "We'll cross examine him to confirm this. Have you ever heard the name Cee Kephart?"

He slides that question in so smoothly, I hardly notice. He studies my face, testing me for cracks.

"No," I lie, and my voice comes out right. It doesn't get small, like it used to. I've gotten better at that.

He keeps going, "She's around your age, you never met someone by that name at school?"

I shake my head.

He moves on. "How about the name Markai Davis?"

"No."

"Maddison Shaw?"

"No."

"Rory Renaud?"

He threw her in there on purpose, trying to trip me up. It works, I pause.

"Yes."

He taps at his screen some more. "How do you know Rory?"

It's a pointless question. He already knows the answer, that's why he's mentioned her.

"We were childhood friends."

"Good friends?" His eyes squint even more, if that's possible.

"Yes."

I wait for him to mention Corinne. That's what he's getting at, isn't it?

"Were you aware that Rory is in a coma?"

My throat tightens further, but the numbness

is right there, and I reach for it, pulling it around me like a comforting fog, relying on it to get me through. The same thing I've been doing ever since I saw her in that bed at home, slowly dying.

Already dead, in a way.

"Yes."

"How does that make you feel?"

His tone of voice makes it sound like the test questions Corinne used on me, back at the clinic for my check-up. The test I failed.

I try not to deviate from the truth, without revealing too much. "It's unfortunate."

His voice goes up a notch in volume. "Have you experienced any drastic emotions regarding your friend's situation?"

"No."

His voice goes up again. "Have you experienced any drastic emotions regarding the cure and what it has done to your friend?"

I recognize what he's doing. He's digging for a motive, a reason I might get involved in any resistance efforts.

I keep my voice even. "No."

"Have you or anyone you know participated in any resistance efforts against the current government?"

He's almost shouting now, his voice rising from

low in his abdomen, his throat bobbing with the effort. I wonder if they teach this at peacekeeper school, if it's an interrogation method meant to apply pressure on the subject, or if it's something he learned all on his own.

Maybe he's not as harmless as he seems.

I'm surprised I'm able to stay calm, but I guess I've gotten good at regulating my emotions. Every day since the cure has been a test, a practice. This isn't all that different.

I tell him the truth. "I would never participate in any acts of terrorism."

He leans back in his chair. I'm thinking he's satisfied with my answer, but then he throws in something completely unexpected. "How much do you know about your biological father?"

I frown. I can't help it. "Nothing."

Thankfully, he doesn't appear alarmed by my reaction. "Your father was an active participant in known rebel groups. You've never had any contact with him?"

I shake my head, not trusting my voice.

The peacekeeper reads something on his tablet. "Says here he committed suicide seven years ago, after serving five years of his sentence at the rehabilitation penitentiary. It says that any attempts to cure him had failed."

Seven years ago. The same year as my mother.

Maybe that's why she did it. She couldn't stand to live in a world without him. The possibility enters my mind in a flash, whole and compact. It would make perfect sense, wouldn't it?

But of course, I'll never know for sure.

"You never had any contact with him during his sentencing?" the peacekeeper asks.

I need to say something now, I can't keep giving non-answers. "We never knew anything about him, and I don't remember him from my early childhood."

I'm relieved none of my emotions appear to be breaking through the surface.

On the inside, I'm spinning. No wonder I had one of the top-ranking peacekeepers assigned to my household—no wonder I was one of the first people to be cured—no wonder I'm being interrogated now.

Three suicides in one family.

The curse runs deep, and I'm the last one left.

"When you say we, are you referring to your twin sister?" he asks, forcing my attention back to the present.

"Sara, yes."

"You found her?"

"In the bathroom," I say. "We didn't even know she was sick."

"You never suspected that you might be sick also, Sabine?"

I look him straight in his squinty eyes. "Never."

For long minutes, he doesn't do or say anything. Then finally he nods, reaches across the table, and clicks the recorder off, neat as a punctuation mark. The interrogation is over.

20

Two weeks later, there's a book sitting on my desk at work. It's a prayer book—neat and small, easy to carry. The cover is a soft blue, like the healer outfits. Innocent until opened.

My heart beats faster, my instincts kicking in, sensing danger. Even though it's just a book.

I don't open it. Instead, I push it aside and run through my usual morning tasks, ignoring the burn of curiosity in the pit of my stomach. A part of me doesn't want to acknowledge the book at all, since I'd rather avoid these games.

At lunch, I reluctantly carry the thing with me and pretend to be reading between bites of my sandwich. All I'm really doing is flipping through and scanning the pages, searching for an explanation. There are soft pencil marks underlining certain words, so faint I almost miss them. I don't have the time to decipher it, but there's definitely a message hidden in here. A reminder that someone knows my truth—*a threat.*

The little book feels heavy in my pocket when

I walk back to my desk after lunch, and I know I won't be able to avoid this forever.

They know I'm not cured.

The girl with the black bob, the one I've learned is named Sloane, still works in the building and our paths cross daily. Our eyes will meet, and I'll get this uncomfortable feeling, like she's trying to silently warn me of something. Same thing with George, if we pass each other on the street, those brooding dark eyes cutting straight through.

After Alexei left, I thought the worst was over. What more could they want? But Sloane evidently dropped this on my desk for me to find, which means there's more.

$$\triangle\triangle\triangle$$

At home that evening, I wait for my stepfather to leave for church. He has rehearsals, since he joined the choir, filling in for the new vacancies.

The peacekeeper goes with him.

I wait a few minutes after they've left, before shuffling to the study. I close the door firmly shut. Standing in this room, I remember Alexei behind this desk, his head bent over his work, shiny metallic blonde, the shelves of books all around.

There's a lingering sadness when I sit in the same seat as him, his absence an ever-present ghost in the house.

I force myself to focus, pulling a clean sheet of paper and a pen from one of the drawers. I set the little prayer book flat on the desk's surface, tentatively cracking it open, as though afraid of unleashing whatever awaits within.

I'm careful not to miss any of the pencil marks as I flip through, marking each word on my blank sheet of paper.

Once finished, I flatten the paper to inspect it. Words sit on the page, as harmless as words can be, but they seem to scream at me in their black ink.

"We will come find you. Be ready."

If they mean to frighten me, it's worked. I slam the prayer book shut. I contemplate burning it in the fireplace, as though the book itself is responsible. With shaking hands, I crumple the page and throw it in the paper shredder.

The machine eats the words, scrambling them forever.

Once finished, I lean backwards into the soft leather of the chair and try to remember how to breathe. I feel strangely untethered without a peacekeeper in the house. More exposed. Not that long ago, I'd desperately wanted them all gone, with their gloomy black coats, suffocating us with their version of protection.

It's stupid to want it back—one peacekeeper, in

particular—and I wonder at what point did things change so drastically? What was the defining moment that turned everything inside out? I can't even remember. It seemed to have happened in an instant, and yet in a combination of moments, until the enemy shapeshifted before my eyes.

It's my allies, George and the uncured, who betrayed me. And this little prayer book promises more to come.

21

On Sunday, we walk to church. We stand in the pews like everyone else, and I light my candles like I'm supposed to. Maybe I should light three, one for my biological father, but I don't.

There are less peacekeepers among us now. Only a few black coats. The squinty-eyed one is already gone, now we've proven not to be a threat.

They're moving on, curing people in a different place.

It's while walking back to my seat to rejoin my stepfather that my eye catches on a familiar face in the crowd.

I didn't expect anything on a Sunday. Not during a service. The prayer book should have been a clue, but I never made the connection.

George won't take his eyes off me, but I act like I don't notice him, quietly resuming my spot next to my stepfather.

Except his presence still looms at my back.

When the service ends and everyone stands, I steal a glance behind me, and George points to the floor.

The basement.

When the church doors open, a rush of fresh air pours in and everyone starts filing out, people crowding the aisles. George's tall figure disappears among them.

I turn to my stepfather. "I'll meet you back at home."

"Where are you going?"

"I just have to go to the bathroom real quick. Go ahead, I'll catch up."

He nods and I break away from the crowd, heading towards the stairs.

The basement of the church houses a community hall, but today all the tables are folded and stacked against the walls, leaving nothing but a large vacant space, old and forgotten. Dust clings to every surface and an old ceiling lamp softly buzzes overhead.

I don't see anyone, but the faint aroma of cigarettes clings to the air, growing stronger near the back of the room, where the bathrooms are.

Chills break out over my arms. The further away I get from the exits, the more claustrophobic I feel. If they try anything, I'll be trapped, but I have no choice. They're not going to let this go.

Cee is the one standing by the sinks, but Markai can't be far. I hang by the door, reluctant to go any further, even though I'm pretty sure it won't help any.

The lights in here are soft, muted. As if they want this space to occupy the same tranquility as the rest of the building. The walls and floors are matte black, the mirrors are surrounded by shimmery lights, painting the room a gentle blueish.

Cee doesn't look up as she washes her hands. Her brown hair is scraped back against her scalp extra tightly, but she runs her wet hands over it, flattening it further, and when wet, it takes on a hint of electric blue in this light.

Whereas mine maintains its stubborn red.

In the mirror, her gaze collides with mine. Seeing our reflections side by side like this, our differences stand out starkly. Her edges are sharp where mine are soft. Her eyebrows are dark stabs above a strong pair of eyes, steady and determined as the rest of her, her jawbone and shoulders jutting out, as though bracing herself for a fight.

"We need to talk."

"About what?"

"You know what." She turns off the tap, flicks the water onto the floor, little drops scattering across the tiles.

The gesture seems especially insulting, in a

church.

Someone clears their throat from just outside the door, letting us know they're here. *Markai.*

I'm trapped.

"How much did you tell them?" Cee asks.

"I didn't tell them anything."

"Am I supposed to believe that?" She smiles but it looks like a grimace. "*That peacekeeper* didn't show up, so you must have told him something. All I need to know is how much."

The way she says it—*that peacekeeper*—you can hear the hatred.

I prickle defensively. "You guys told me to keep quiet, so I did."

She ignores that. "I know you didn't give them our meeting spot. The peacekeepers would have raided it by now. But we're being watched, so you gave up some names."

I shake my head. "All I did was stop Alexei from getting to the bridge on time. I didn't even tell him why."

She winces slightly at his name, then her eyes narrow. "Don't lie."

The door bangs open and the smell of smoke wafts over to me. Markai steps forward, his reflection joining ours in the mirror, long hair still clinging to the sides of his face, slightly damp with a natural greasiness, unruly brows knit tight together. "This is taking too long. Is she not talking?"

"Give her another minute," Cee says.

Caught between them, I laugh, mostly from nerves. "What? What do you think you're going to do?"

They've already proven they're not above blowing people up.

Markai cracks his knuckles, and I want to laugh again. The tension is getting to my head.

"My stepfather will be waiting at home," I say. "He'll notice if I don't come back soon."

Cee shrugs. "I'm sure we can come up with an excuse for that."

Despite everything else going on, these are the words that worry me the most. *They're really not going to let me walk out of here, are they?*

Markai speaks next. "George assured us you were meant to be a part of the group, so we chose to trust you."

I look at him, my voice taking on an edge of desperation. "I didn't say anything, to anyone."

"Then why are we being followed?" Cee snaps at me, teeth flashing. "How do they know who to look for?"

I'm getting annoyed. "I don't know, maybe because you blew up a bridge?"

Cee's brows twitch up her forehead and I know I've said the wrong thing. She nods her head to Markai, and he moves on me fast, latching his hand around my arm, twisting it hard. I don't expect it to hurt as much as it does, my skin pinched and stinging in his grip, his fingers wrapping snugly around the bone.

My arm seems awfully delicate, all of a sudden. Like he could snap it with his big hand. His wrist looks double the size of mine.

He hadn't seemed this scary, the first time I met him. Maybe because George was there. George makes everyone look smaller, in comparison.

Markai's other hand comes forward, palm up. "Take your tablet out."

I do as I'm asked, reaching into my pocket and pulling out my personal tablet. The glass feels thin and fragile, despite being my only weapon—my only chance to call someone if this goes seriously wrong.

"Send a message to your stepfather that you're going to be home late. Show me the message when you're done."

I stare at the device in my palm and the room tilts. They're leaving me no choice. My thumb slides over the screen, opening the messaging app and typing out a few words. Markai watches from over my shoulder until I've pressed send.

Then he takes the device from me. I'm left clutching air—my last chance for help slipping through my fingers.

"Where are we going?" I ask.

Neither of them answers.

△△△

They take me to the blue house where we first met, down to the room with the single light-bulb. They put me in a chair and bind my hands together with a rope. It digs into my skin and threatens to cut off my circulation. My fingers feel fuzzy after just a few minutes.

Cee is more composed, but Markai is pacing, his thumb in his mouth so he can chew on the nail.

The fear is starting to dissipate, replaced with something more like anger. "If I'd told anyone, they would have arrested you."

Markai continues to pace. Cee checks her smart-watch and her eyes dart to the door.

"Are we waiting for someone?" I ask, but again, no one answers.

A patch of sunlight slants through the window, sliding down the wall as time passes. The two of them sit at the other end of the table, going over pages, shuffling and rustling them. Paper is harder to track than technology.

They make sure I can't see what they're doing, keeping everything angled just right.

It must be several hours before there's the sound of a truck outside, wheels on gravel, followed by a door slamming shut. All three of us turn towards the noise. Heavy footsteps come down the stairs, and when the door opens, it's George. He looks impossibly tall down here, he has to duck a little.

His head of thick hair and his dark eyes are exactly as they always have been, and my heart clenches. How did I end up here like this? How can your enemy wear the face of a boy you once loved?

Rory comes to mind. What would she say, if she saw him right now, keeping me prisoner?

George at least has the decency to look sorry, his eyes cast to the floor.

"Is it all ready?" Cee asks him, and he nods.

They might be talking about me, they might not. Nothing more is said aloud, but I already know it's something bad.

George turns towards me, meeting my eye for the first time. When he steps into the light, I can see a vein in his temple, pulsing softly. Perspiration clings to his forehead and he runs his hand over, to wipe away the evidence.

It makes me nervous, seeing him nervous.

Markai leans in the corner and lights a cigarette with a match. He drops the match to the floor and kills the flame with his boot.

Right now, I feel like that flame, getting crushed under his foot.

I shuffle uncomfortably in my seat, and Markai's mouth twitches, like he enjoys seeing me squirm. My wrists ache in their bindings.

I glance up at George. "What are you planning to do?"

"We can't have you sabotaging things again." He manages to keep his voice even, his expression flat. It's not that hard of a trick. Anyone who is used to pretending to be cured can pull that off.

"But I don't even know anything," I say uselessly.

"We know you talked," Cee says. Now we're both repeating ourselves. A pair of broken records, us two. "All we need are the names you gave."

I guess that's why I'm here. They need to know who is compromised and who isn't. Which means they must be planning something else—another attack?

George leans closer, his eyes sad. "Please, Sabine."

"I'm telling the truth," I say.

Markai groans. "Enough of this."

He drops the cigarette and stubs that out, too. One slam of his boot, and I feel myself shrink. He moves forward in a cloud of smoke, the awful scent of it filling my nose, and pushes George out of the way.

He does it fast. Raising his hand and slapping me across the face in a single, clean motion. I rattle in my chair, a gasp ripping from my throat. The impact stings, but only for a second. Then my cheeks burn hot, although it might be from embarrassment more than anything.

George whips toward Markai and shoves him backwards, one arm pinned against his chest. "What the hell!"

Markai just pushes him off and laughs his awful laugh, the sound of it booming off the walls. "We've already tried asking her nicely."

George places himself between the two of us. "I don't think that's necessary."

I stare at them all. This is something else. These people aren't just uncured. Markai looks like he might have the sickness, like he might be on the edge. George looks defeated, as if he knows they've gone too far, but I guess there's no going back for him. Cee looks determined to the point of obsession.

Together, they make a very dangerous team, and a small part of me feels like maybe the government is right—maybe human beings need to be cured.

Just maybe not the way they're doing it.

George brushes himself off, attempts to calm down. He looks at me with those rich eyes of his. "Why did you do it? You ruined our one chance."

I shake my head. "All I did was stop him from leaving—stop him from getting to the bridge on time."

"Yes." He's pretending to believe me. "But why? You saw what they did to Rory."

It's a low blow but I hold my ground. "Yes, I've seen her."

"Then how could you?"

It's important for me to explain myself, I can see that. At least to George. Markai looks bored, and Cee looks like she's already offended by my answer, regardless of what it might be.

I take a breath, shuffling the words in my mind, trying to make them fit in the right order. "I have to hold on to whatever humanity I have left."

George is the one who looks offended, in the end.

Cee just sneers. "What did they promise you? Did they offer you something in exchange for information?"

She still doesn't believe me.

"I think she's telling the truth," George says

after a moment, his voice small. I've never heard him sound so small. I thought he was incapable of it.

"You," Markai hisses, pointing an accusatory finger at George, "you're the reason we're in this mess in the first place. You promised she could be trusted."

George opens his mouth to retort but Cee cuts them both off.

"We're running out of time here, guys."

I check the spot of sunlight on the wall. There's just a sliver of it left, glowing in a soft shade of pink. It's getting late, it'll be dark soon.

"You think we should go ahead? Even though…" Markai doesn't finish, just looks at me.

I'm starting to piece things together. "You're trying to leave the collective?"

All three of them turn in my direction. Cee shoots a glare at Markai, as if it's his fault I figured it out.

It makes sense. They need to know who can safely make it through the checkpoints. You can't get through without scanning your identification card, and if you've been flagged in the system, peacekeepers will immediately come pick you up.

That's why I've been brought here.

22

Outside, dusk has begun to fall. George has pulled up a chair close to mine. I can tell he feels sorry about this.

Cee and Markai have left and come back a couple of times. They're sitting at the table again, with their papers, only this time I can tell one of them is a map, but that's the most I get a glimpse at.

Markai has smoked another three cigarettes, but only halfway, and he keeps flattening them to the floor when he's finished. It's as if he wants to leave evidence.

I turn to George, holding up my hands. My wrists are still wrapped in rope and my fingers have turned an unsettling shade of white. It's been like this for so long, I can scarcely feel them anymore. I've tried wiggling them to keep a little circulation going, but too much moving only makes the rope bite deeper, ready to tear the skin.

"How much longer are you guys going to keep me tied up like this?" I ask.

George ignores the question, as though afraid of it.

I try something else. "My stepfather must be worried."

"We'll take you home as soon as it's dark out," Cee says from across the room. She's getting impatient, too. She's been glancing at her smart-watch every few seconds, like a nervous tick.

The mounting anxiety is getting to all of us.

Finally, there's the familiar strike of the match from across the room, and I expect Markai is lighting up again, but this time he's got the flame aimed at the pile of papers. I watch the fire dance as he makes them all burn, erasing their plans from existence.

They've been studying them all afternoon. Committing them to memory, I realize.

Cee glances at her smart-watch again. "You can take her to the truck, George. We'll be behind you in a minute."

We do as we're told. On our way up the stairs, we cross paths with Sloane. She looks at George, but never at me.

"Has she talked?" she asks, but when he says nothing, she laughs. "I guess not."

"You're just on time," he says.

She nods. "I was told not to come a minute

sooner."

She continues down, while we go up. Outside, the night air is cool brushing against my skin. George guides me to the truck, one of the generic models. Most vehicles look alike, but this has to be one of the most common ones.

They're making sure not to stand out.

George opens the hatch into the back and helps me in. Sideways seating and black-tinted windows. The two seats at the end are crowded with stuff, luggage and supplies it looks like, so I settle into the next available spot. My hands are shaking inside their bindings.

"We're going to take you home," George promises, but the way he keeps saying it makes me think they aren't.

He buckles me in, because I can't do it myself, then gives me a brief squeeze of the shoulder, a silent apology. I know he's only doing that for Rory's benefit, so I don't thank him.

Cee and Sloane show up soon after. They all climb in and shut the hatch, which means Markai must be in front. I can't actually see him, because the partition is shut.

After a minute, the truck starts with a sigh, almost completely silent, undetectable in the night.

My heart drums against my ribcage. I can't

shake the feeling they're not going to let me go.

Once we're on the road, Cee nods to George. "You can untie her."

I guess she doesn't think I'll risk jumping from a moving car. She happens to be right.

George cuts the rope with a pocketknife and I actually gasp from the relief, quickly rubbing my sore wrists. The skin is red and raw, close to bleeding.

George drops the rope to the floor, like he's ashamed of it. It coils at our feel like a snake going to sleep, its job done.

I study the tinted windows, trying to make sense of where we are and where we're going, but it's practically impossible to make sense of anything. We're going too fast, everything outside is a dark blur with no shapes.

I can tell when we've been driving for too long, though. "You're not taking me home."

Cee glances at me. "We can't let you out here, someone might see. We'll let you out a little further."

George frowns. "That's not what you said."

The uncertainty in his voice should alarm me, but I'm calm instead, resigned.

Cee smiles, a fake one. "It's safer this way. For all of us."

Sloane still hasn't acknowledged me. Does she know something? No one wants to look their victim in the eye, if they can avoid it.

I turn a pair of accusatory eyes onto George, but he just pats my knee, like that's going to help.

A spit of anger flares inside me. "Just let me out, Cee."

Her expression goes blank. That rehearsed smoothness all uncureds are used to wearing. "No."

"Just let her out," George fights for me. "It's late, there's no one around to see."

"It's passed curfew. She'll get caught and she'll probably tell them everything, just like she did last time."

I grit my teeth together. "I never told them anything."

This time, the corner of her mouth turns up. "I guess we'll find out when we get to the checkpoint."

We hit a bump, which sends us jostling in the back, knees bumping. The panic slams into me so hard and so suddenly, I almost throw up—almost spill all my nerves right onto the floor.

"Cee." George is still trying to reason with her. "I don't think we nee—"

"This is your fault, too." She narrows her eyes at

him. "If we go down, she goes down with us."

Sloane is actually smiling, all serene-like, not a care in the world, and I feel a chill scratching at my spine.

George leans back into his seat. "I'm sorry," he whispers, so low I hardly catch it.

Outside, the road has changed. It feels rougher. We must be headed away from the main roads.

I stare at my hands in my lap, small and helpless. They still feel fuzzy from the hours of low circulation, like they're still not quite attached to me, but at least they've started to return to a more normal color.

With nothing left to do, I think of my life. All the pieces come together in my mind, the many people who helped shape who I am. My parents and Sara. Rory and Corinne.

I think of my stepfather, too. He offered me a home when I didn't have one, and although he was always a quiet presence, he was a secure one.

Of course, there's Alexei. The image of him is sharp in my mind, all pointy around the edges, like a weapon.

Falling for the enemy, that says a lot about a person, but I don't regret it. I only regret not saying goodbye when I had the chance. Instead, I stood like a petulant child at the window and watched him leave, as if that would somehow make him stay.

I try to imagine things had turned out differently—try to imagine if we lived in a different world. I picture what the moment would have been like, if I'd gone outside, chased him down the path. How do you say goodbye to someone like that? I try to fill in those blanks, the words I didn't say.

My mind is just on the edge of it, the words are within reach, I can see their outline in the darkness.

I love you.

But then the truck suddenly lurches to a stop, jolting us in our seats, and the words are ripped away.

The partition slams open and Markai's voice reaches us in the back. "There's a peacekeeper blocking the road."

In a split second, Cee is already unbuckled and reaching under the seats for something. "Just one?"

"Just one."

She pulls an object out and it flashes silver in the dark. I know what it is instantly, even though I've never seen one up close before, only in movies.

It's a gun.

I gape at the thing and wonder how they've

managed to find one. It must be old, they've gone out of production a long time ago.

She tucks the weapon into the back of her pants and pulls her shirt over, keeping it close but out of sight. "George, you get out first. I've got your back."

He does as he's told—I guess we know where his true loyalty lies—and moves towards the hatch, throwing it open and stepping out into the night. The cold air blows in, a big rush of it sweeping against my face, smelling of forest. Dampness and moss.

There's nothing out there but a long dark road and thick woods on either side. This is the road that leads to the checkpoint in the outskirts of the collective.

Cee hangs by the door, ready to make a move. I unbuckle myself to get a closer look, but I don't get far. Sloan throws her arm out to stop me, clotheslining me hard across the chest. It's the first time she's acknowledged my presence.

George only takes a few steps before we hear the peacekeeper's voice, cutting through the night.

"Stop there," the voice commands. "Hands up."

Chills run up and down my arms. I recognize him immediately.

I don't know who I'm afraid for, but I'm afraid.

George lifts his arms, as instructed, and turns

half a circle to face the voice. Seeing him like that, so exposed, I feel a surge of protectiveness —a surge of pity. George is one of my remaining connections to Rory, now that she's slipped away from us. The love she had for him, and that I once had for him, make it impossible for me to hate him.

It's the only reason I kept quiet, the reason I didn't tell Alexei everything.

George and Rory have melded together in my mind, their love uniting them. I know everything he does is for her.

So it might as well be Rory herself standing out there on the road.

In the dark, there's the rising sound of boots approaching, until Alexei finally steps into my line of vision, and it's like the world bottoms out, seeing the two of them head to head. Alexei's got one hand on his holster, the paralyzer gun at the ready. His eyes quickly assess each of us, one by one. When they land on me, I suck in a sharp breath, but he doesn't linger.

Cee is still hanging by the door, her hand inching towards the back of her shirt.

"Look," George says, trying his best to sound authoritative, "we don't want to hurt you."

Alexei ignores that and gestures ahead, towards the checkpoint. "They're waiting for you."

There's a beat of silence. The wind picks up and whips at us. Alexei's black coat fills like a sail, clapping like a cape. Even sitting inside the truck, I shudder.

George plants his feet, his brow lowering to cast dark shadows over his eyes. "What?"

"They know you're coming. If you keep going, you'll be arrested."

George looks unsure. All he does is shake his head.

Cee starts to climb out of the truck, one hand still near the gun, her frame visibly twitching with impatience. Her feet hit the ground with a smack and she sticks her chin out. "What are you talking about?"

All three of them are now standing on the road, like three points of a triangle.

Alexei faces her. "You're headed into a trap."

"Why should we believe that?"

"I'm just trying to help."

"We thought you were cured," George speaks up, trying to sound defensive, in control, but there's an edge to it—a weak edge. Like he feels guilty and he wants to redeem himself for what they did—for what they tried to do to him.

Alexei cuts a glance in his direction, blue eyes taking on that sharpness that they do, even in the dark. "To be honest, I'm not sure the cure is real."

The rest of us fall silent, struck by this confession, but Cee only barks a laugh. "Even so, why would *you* help us?"

He breaks eye contact with George and looks up into the truck, at me. "I'm not here for you."

With a rush of determination, I shove Sloan out of the way and climb down from the truck, but the second my feet hit the road, Cee whips towards me.

The mood changes in a quick instant—a sharp curve into different territory. I'm not sure what she thought—that I was making a move or what —but her face twists, caught between a sneer and something else, her eyes taking on that usual mania of hers. She reaches for the gun, but she's too slow, untrained. Alexei is like a machine. In a flash, he has the paralyzer raised and aimed at her chest, a little red dot glowing through the dark, marking the spot.

Cee freezes. From my angle, I can see the outline of the gun beneath the fabric of her shirt and her hand wrapped around the handle, fingers tight.

"Alexei," I hiss, a warning.

He doesn't react. He's got his sights locked on Cee, on her arm held behind her back, and his finger held over the trigger.

"Alexei, don't," I try again. "Please."

There's still no reaction, not yet. Long seconds tick by.

Finally, something in his expression unravels. Slowly, almost too slowly, his muscles begin to uncoil, like a hunter moving in reverse.

"They didn't hurt you?" he asks.

"I'm fine."

As soon as the words have left my mouth, he takes his finger off the trigger and draws the paralyzer gun back, replacing it in its hostler.

Time slams to a standstill. I push my way forward, and this time, no one tries to stop me.

When I glance in her direction, Cee is frowning, as though she doesn't understand—as though she can't believe I've disarmed the enemy with nothing but words.

George is quicker to recover. He grabs for my arm when I pass, pulling me to a stop. "Where are you going?"

His voice cracks.

I plant my feet, resisting against his powerful grip. "I'm not going with you."

He blinks slow, a mixture of confusion and surprise, as though seeing me for the first time. He probably is, and I feel a pang of pity for him.

"Let me go, George."

He doesn't. We struggle for a second, and in the

corner of my eye, Alexei reaches for his holster again.

This time, Cee has enough time to pull the gun out, and the sound of the shot is like a bomb going off in the night, thunderous and powerful, clapping against our eardrums.

23

Nobody moves. I forget how to breathe. Panicking, I search for where Alexei's been shot, waiting for the inevitable to happen, but there's no blood, no trace of pain. He's not even moving. Then I notice he's looking at the ground, and I follow his line of sight.

The shot landed on the road. She missed him by inches.

Did she miss her shot, blinded by panic, or did she do it on purpose? Did she just want to scare us?

I suck in big gulps of air, relief shuddering through me, and rip free from George's grip. He doesn't try to resist this time. I slip away effortlessly and cross the remaining distance to Alexei, placing myself between him and the others, as though I'm the protector now.

Alexei reaches out and draws me close, as though it's the most natural thing—as though everything is shifting into its proper place.

When I glance behind me one final time, Cee is watching us with wide eyes. She's dropped her hand to her side, the gun still held in it. From the look of her, I'd say it was the fear that made her pull the trigger.

"They'll be coming now," Alexei warns. "You need to move quickly, if you don't want to get caught."

Cee just nods, the shock still frozen on her face.

No one stops us as we turn away and face the night.

△△△

We walk fast, with nothing but the strips on the road to guide us. When headlights appear on the horizon ahead, Alexei grabs me and pulls us into the trees. We press ourselves into the shadows and wait for the car to pass.

It drives slow, close to a crawl. Whoever is inside is shooting flashlights into the night, clearly searching for something. They've definitely heard the gunshot.

I don't know what's going to happen to the others, but I can't worry about them now.

We tuck ourselves behind a tree and Alexei holds me tight against him. My ear is pressed against his ribcage, and through the layers of clothing I can hear the drumming of his heart.

The beam of the flashlight cuts the dark. The

fuzzy glow of it wraps around the edges of every tree and bush, hunting for its prey.

When the beam hits our spot, every muscle in my body tightens. I hear Alexei stop breathing.

It feels like a long time—too long—before the light shifts away again.

I don't exhale until the car has moved on, my muscles cramped from staying still. I start to pull away, but Alexei locks his arms around me.

"Wait," he whispers.

I do as I'm told. After a second, I can make out the sound of footsteps. Someone is still out there.

It's hard to tell which direction they're coming from, since I have to strain to hear over the rushing in my head, but there's no flashlight this time, so maybe it's not a peacekeeper—maybe it's one of the rebels.

The sound of the footsteps rises and then fades.

Alexei still has me pressed against him, his body heat keeping me warm against the cold night. We wait an extra minute, just to be safe, and finally we unfreeze. He clutches my hand in his big one and we hurry back to the road, walking as quickly as we can.

The crunch of the dirt beneath my boots is startling, like it might give us away, and we don't talk, too afraid of anyone else being out there. The forest feels like it's full of monsters, and I keep picturing eyes in the dark, glowing as they watch us.

Except when I check, there's nothing.

We come to a fork in the road and Alexei steers us to the left. He picks up the pace and I struggle to keep up, exhaustion clinging to my limbs, all the emotions of the day catching up to me.

Ahead of us, a black car materializes in the dark, parked on the side of the road. Alexei drops my hand and reaches into his pocket for something. He presses a button and the car unlocks.

We're moving fast now, Alexei is rushing me forward, his hand at my back. Safety is within reach. There isn't time for anything else.

He opens the door. "Get in."

I hesitate, suddenly breathless. This is too fast. Our time together is already ending, slipping through my fingers like silk, and I'm left scrambling—trying to recover, trying to hold onto what few precious seconds I have.

"Where are you going now?"

"I have to go back."

I don't know how to tell him I can't bear to see him walk away, so all I manage is, "I thought you were gone."

He lets out a slow breath. "I know. I'm sorry. I thought if I disappeared, they'd leave you alone."

He pushes the key fob in my palm. My hand

shakes as it closes around it, and I look up at him.

"You're safe now," he says. "The car can take you home."

My voice gets small again. It hasn't done that in a while. "What about you?"

Somehow, he hears me. Maybe he's gotten used to it. "I told you, I have to go back."

"But will we see each other again?"

All around us, the night is pure stillness. I just got him back and he's already leaving.

He shakes his head. "I think it's better if we don't."

"You won't come back this time, will you?"

"Everything's going to be alright, Sabine," he says, but it doesn't feel that way. He didn't even answer my question.

I look away, refusing to get into the car. I'm not trying to be unfair, but I've never been good at goodbyes. Everyone I've ever cared about has left me, usually in the most horrible of ways—usually without any words. I don't know how to do this.

"I have to go," he says. He keeps saying it, but it doesn't make it any easier. "It could be really bad, for both of us, if we're caught together."

Now that we're at the end, I find myself remembering the beginning. I'd gone to work, like any other day, and then come home to find him already moved in. He'd acted like he belonged there, like he'd been a part of the furniture all along and we had simply not noticed. Then there were those silent first dinners around the table, sitting rigid in our seats, knowing he was watching.

I'm here for your protection. It's my job to look after you. When he was saying these things, did they mean something else? Something more?

Or is that just wishful thinking?

Finally, I look at him, searching.

"I hope you know," he says, his voice dropping even lower, "how I feel."

Do I? I study his face, blue eyes cutting through the darkness.

"I'll come back for you someday," he says.

It's a promise and I hold it close. It's all I have. Then I watch him go into the dark, boots marching the ground, black coat fading into the night.

I climb into the backseat of the car, and when the door swoops shut, it's the sound of an ending. I curl up onto the seat, feeling tired and hollow. The spot next to me is vacant, and I stare into it. The emptiness is loud, filling the car, impossible to ignore. An absence that clings to you like a phantom with outstretched claws.

The car starts to drive off, rolling softly over the uneven road, and all that's left for me to do is go home and wait. Today, and tomorrow, and the day after, that's what I'll be doing. I'll be waiting. It seems I've been doing a lot of that lately, waiting for Alexei, and perhaps waiting is my new curse, but I don't mind so much.

I've been cursed with worse things.

X

It isn't until months later that Rory's face shows up on the newsfeeds, attached to a time of death and an announcement for the scheduled funeral services.

THE END

EXCERPT | SEASON 2

The cure for mental illness has existed for a long time, but it was never enforced.
Until now.

I left my family and my hometown eight years ago, to pursue a career as a healer. I honestly thought I was going to help cure the world. Four years of medical school, that's what they promised. That we were going to help make the world a better place.

But you can't be a healer if you're not cured yourself.

It wasn't what I expected. The cure. It felt like the life had been sucked out of me. I could still remember what I felt like before, but that version of myself was suddenly gone. Like going from fully alive to only half alive.

After that, I thought they'd taken everything there was to take from me. **I was wrong.**

HEALER | 1

T he day of my sister's funeral is bright. Unbearably bright. Insultingly bright.

My parents are here, although it would be just as accurate to say they aren't here at all. The cure does that to people. It steals their soul straight out of their bones—if that is in fact where the soul lives, embedded in our skeletons—and leaves behind an empty shell. It's a kind of vacancy that invades you, an emptiness that grows.

The emptiness inside me feels like that, but it isn't because of the cure. It's because of grief.

The funeral parlor is all white walls and glass, little fountains of slow trickling water. The space is supposed to seem peaceful, but I feel anything but peaceful, standing among the friends and family that have come to commemorate Rory's pitifully short life.

A small service, people sharing memories. Sandwiches laid out with paper plates and napkins, lemon water in plastic cups. It all seems so inadequate, I could scream. I can feel it building in the pit of my stomach. The ceilings in here are high, I bet it would make an amazing echo, the scream bouncing around up there.

It was supposed to be temporary, me coming home. I'd avoided coming home for eight years, but then I'd heard the news: my little sister was in a coma. As a trained healer, I was granted a work transfer and shipped back to my hometown on the next flight out. The new law had just been passed, enforcing all citizens to receive the cure for mental illness, and there was a high demand for healers like me.

I'd never intended to stay. It's been one of the hardest things I've had to do, which seems strange to say, since the act of staying isn't really an action at all. It's the opposite, it means doing nothing, but I never felt like I belonged here in Reye. Rory was supposed to wake up and resume her rightful place as the daughter who didn't abandon her family, and the curing efforts were supposed to take six weeks. That's what they predicted.

Then three months went by, followed by another three. Nothing went according to plan.

I don't actually know when we stopped waiting for Rory to wake up and started waiting for her to die. Now there's an urn on the shelf over there, reminding us she's gone for good, and every time I look at it, it feels like a piece of myself has been ripped out.

I bet Rory doesn't feel at peace, her ashes stuffed in that thing. A long time ago, the deceased were buried, and I wish we still did that. I wish it was still an option, at least. Maybe it would be better, to be put in the ground to become a part of the earth.

But then again, maybe not. They would put you in a box, wouldn't they? So you didn't really become part of the earth at all. And isn't a box just as bad as an urn? You're still confined. What if your immortal soul can't escape no matter how hard you bang and scrape against the lid? Would it feel like suffocating forever?

I feel like I'm suffocating right now, just thinking about it. It doesn't help that I'm wearing a stupid itchy dress, all black with a frilly collar that keeps scraping against my throat like the claws of a cat. It looked brand new hanging in Rory's closet, like she'd never worn it, and now I understand why. I keep tugging on the collar when I think no one is looking, hoping to relieve the itchiness, but it doesn't help much.

A part of me feels like an impostor, wearing her dress, but I hadn't packed funeral clothes. I didn't think there was a need, and in retrospect, that seems awfully hopeful of me. Embarrassingly so.

At least there's something comforting about wearing her clothes, as if it's a way of keeping her close—a way of keeping her alive. She was the same age I was when I left home. Eighteen years old, a whole future ahead. I feel guilty, like I've somehow stolen years from her simply by living longer, and it makes my eyes burn.

I force back the tears. People don't cry when they're cured, not even if someone you love has died. It seems wrong, of course. Unnatural. How can they do this to us? Take the humanity straight out? The more people I see being cured, the more unsettling it feels, but I can't say that out loud.

Healers are at the forefront of the war against mental illness, which means I can't admit to anyone that I have doubts.

I catch someone's eye from across the room—a familiar face. Bronze skin and amber eyes. For a second, I wonder if he's guessed my thoughts and I feel a twinge of panic, but nothing in his expression indicates he has.

Sofian Hunt and his family have come to pay their respects. The Hunts have been our neighbors for years, but Sofian especially has a reason to be here. He was supposed to marry Rory.

He looks different than I remember. Taller, more angular. Although I suppose that comes with age. He offers a polite nod from across the room, and I wonder how he's handling this—I wonder if he's cured.

That's all I seem to think about now. Whenever I meet someone, I make a study of them. Are they faking it or did the cure actually work for them? It's hard to tell. People have gotten good at pretending.

The only way to know for sure is to get them to come to the clinic for a check-up. There's a test we make them take. I'm just glad healers don't have to take the test. It means I'm getting away with it, for now. An uncured hiding in plain sight.

Until they change all the rules again. They like to do that, shuffle all the cards, leave the world scrambling.

I watch Sofian shake my father's hand, saying something I can't hear from this distance, but when they both glance in my direction, I know they're talking about me. I make sure to look away, acting like I didn't notice.

Deep down, my heart aches. I always liked Sofian. I would have loved to see those kids get married. Maybe I would have made the trip home, just to see it. My sister deserved to get her happily ever. If anyone did, it was her. She was the one who believed in those kinds of things. Not me, the cynic.

It seems unfair, that I'm the one who gets to live, when I'm not the one with the dreams.

I move towards the back of the room, hoping to be forgotten for a minute. I tuck myself into a quiet corner and watch people filtering in and out the doors, coming to say their goodbyes to my sister's ashes. Old schoolmates and teachers, friends and distant family.

I don't expect to see a black coat among them.

I blink at him, unsure if I'm seeing him right. The black coat is the uniform of the peacekeepers, a symbol of both protection and terror. This one is tall, a head of shiny gold towering above everyone else, cutting a dark shape among the mourners.

He looks like the grim reaper himself, coming to the funeral to collect.

I have to stifle the shock before it shows up on my face. I've been waiting months for the shoe to drop—for someone to realize I've been falsifying medical documents. Every day, I expect the authorities to come after me.

Maybe today is the day.

I relax when someone else steps through the door, and I realize the peacekeeper isn't alone. He's not here to arrest me.

I recognize Sabine's copper hair first, glinting in the sunlight like strands of gold and fire. I wonder if she resents that bright shade? Red isn't a popular color these days. Marked, you could say.

Sabine was Rory's closest friend, and she walks into the room with her back very straight, her grey eyes flat like still water. No one would suspect she isn't cured. Only I know. I'm the one who falsified her documents.

The whole while I'm watching her, the peace-keeper is at her side, hovering like a shadow. It makes me nervous, seeing him stand so close, when I know the truth about her.

In the early days after the new law was passed, peacekeepers were everywhere, protecting our citizens. Which is just another way of saying they were always watching. But we don't see them so much now that everyone in Reye has been cured, only a few peacekeepers remain, which begs the question: is Sabine being guarded for a reason? Have they found out?

Has she told them about me—about what I did?

The questions swarm around my head like bees, and I have to resist the urge to chew my lip. Cured people don't do that. The trick to appearing cured is in the details, the littlest things will give you away. Don't fidget, don't squirm, don't bite your nails.

I continue to watch Sabine as she stands in line and waits her turn. Finally, she stops in front of Rory's urn, head bowed and eyes closed. She taps the side of her hand and her lips move in silent prayer.

She was one of the first people in town to be cured. It's like they've been keeping an eye on her, more than the others. I've heard the rumors myself, about her family, and I wonder if that's why she's being guarded—because they suspect she's a threat?

Maybe it was too big of a risk, helping her. Maybe I made a mistake.

She finishes praying and walks away, and when she lifts her head, she spots me. I feel pinned in place, exposed. There's nowhere to run.

She crosses the room with the peacekeeper trailing close behind, and with each step of the black coat coming nearer—each stomp of his boots across the floor—my pulse pounds harder in my ears.

SEASON 2 | COMING SOON

ACKNOWLEDGEMENT

So many people attributed to the creation of this book, it's almost impossible to decide where to begin!

First off, I want to kickstart these acknowledgements by mentioning... the lobotomy. The lobotomy was a prime source of inspiration when writing this book, therefore, thank you, precious history, for that little nugget.
Second, shout out to the global pandemic for making my book feel eerily relevant to the times. Although the "disease" in my book is mental illness, I shuddered at the constant echoes of reality tucked within these pages.

As for the lovely humans that endured my endless chatter about books, and who never failed to give my scribblings a read when asked, you are all invaluable assets to my creative process. So big thanks to my mom for being my first fan! (It's not an acknowledgement page without a shoutout to mom.) Thank you to my husband for listening to me rant about my writing process practically every day and for driving me to get Starbucks whenever I needed an extra something to keep me going. Thank you to my darling supportive group of friends and family, including, but not limited to: the badass that is my sister-cousin Catherine, the always inspiring and fellow soul Felix, the adventurous Vanessa and her mom—AKA my very own matante Pauline, who volunteered her proofreading skills like a champ!

And finally, but not least, a big thanks to my three cats for being absolutely no help at all, except to walk across my keyboard at the least opportune moments.

I wouldn't have been able to complete this book without you all!

Much love,
Mags
xox

ABOUT THE AUTHOR

Maggie Ray

 Self-proclaimed struggling artist fueled by Starbucks & pizza, hoarder of books & kitties.

Maggie Ray is a small-business owner living on the East Coast of Canada, where she has been writing fiction and winning book awards for the last fifteen years.

Her book, Daughters of the King, has gained a readership of 60,000+ online, hit #1 on the charts for its genre, and continues to maintain an average 5-star rating on popular online platforms. Her new series, the Uncured, revolves around a cure for mental illness, with each book (affectionally called seasons) featuring a different character.

BOOKS IN THIS SERIES

THE UNCURED SERIES

STAY CONNECTED!

WWW.MRSAUTHOR.COM

Printed in Great Britain
by Amazon

60195368R00132

Citizen

Season 1 | Uncured

Maggie Ray

Copyright © 2020 Maggie Ray

All rights reserved

The characters and events portrayed in this book are fictitious. Any similarity
to real persons, living or dead, is coincidental and not intended by the author.

No part of this book may be reproduced, or stored in a retrieval system,
or transmitted in any form or by any means, electronic, mechanical,
photocopying, recording, or otherwise, without express written permission of
the publisher.

ISBN: 9798697375327
Imprint: Independently published
Cover design by: Maggie Ray